The Arrow Journey

Gerard Mulligan

Whimsical Publications, LLC

Florida

The Arrow Journey is a work of fiction. Names, characters, and incidents are the products of the author's imagination and are either fictitious or are used fictitiously. Any resemblance to actual events or persons, living or dead, is entirely coincidental.

To purchase the authorized electronic edition of *The Arrow Journey*, visit www.whimsicalpublications.com

Cover art by Shyanne England
Editing by Melissa Hosack

ISBN-13: 978-1-940707-96-9

Published by
Whimsical Publications, LLC
Florida

Where was I exactly? Had I not just been in the house? I peered down at the object and saw it was covered in short hairs and now lay still. Had Grandad gotten a dog without telling anyone? After a moment, when my mind caught up with the reality of what my eyes were seeing, I saw in fact that it not an animal but a man who, for whatever reason, was dressed in a dog costume of some sort. Now that he was lying down, I could clearly see his form underneath the costume. He seemed to have stopped cold. To his right, I just then noticed, there was a large stick on fire implanted into the ground.

What was going on? The whole thing must, I thought, be part of a stage play that the man was acting in. The costumes and flaming stick all looked like they came from one of Shakespeare's plays, *King Lear* or one of them, that we had read in school over the years. I stepped around the man, more out of curiosity than for any sane reason, and saw that he had a gash of blood on his forehead. A very realistic bright berry red, I had to admit. There was a boulder protruding from the ground and it almost appeared as if he had fallen and hit his head on that. How, though, had I gone from Grandad's office into a play and, moreover, one that was set outdoors? Had I fallen out one of the windows into the garden? I needed to find out where I was first.

I looked up from the man to see a wooden house with its roof on fire, grey smoke drifting up into a pale blue sky, a short distance away. The house was standing in the middle of a large clearing surrounded by woodland. Perhaps it was not a play after all. Was I on a movie set instead? A girl appeared in front of me. Where had she come from? Had she been hiding in the grass? She was about my age with raven-colored hair cut short and stood up to my shoulder. She was also wearing a strange animal costume. She shouted something I did not understand. She must not speak English, I thought, so maybe she was from abroad. She was very pretty, I noticed. Again, the girl said something, quieter this time, and pointed away from me over my shoulder. I turned around and found another older woman standing there.

"Hello," I said.

Then, behind the older woman, where the ground sloped slightly downward, I saw what the girl was probably really pointing to. A line of men, five or six, likewise dressed in dog costumes, were slowly coming up the incline toward us. I watched them for a few moments. Was it just me or did they seem to be spreading out as they got nearer, as if, almost ridiculously I thought, they were attempting to circle around us. Who were these men?

Everything seemed wrong here. The girl said something once more and reached out to grab my hand to pull me toward her. I stumbled a foot or so in her direction but then remained there in a stunned sort of way trying to figure out what was going on. I just could not understand what she wanted, but I could see she was genuinely scared. She shook her head at me and, releasing me to take the hand of the older woman, they both ran toward the burning house. I watched them as they reached the house and veered off to one side to head for the tree line behind.

Why were they fleeing a movie set? I looked about me again and saw, other than the men who were still getting closer all the while, there was now no one else near me. The only other structure I saw was a timber fence about twenty feet away with two shaggy brown cows who stared at the burning house with detached bovine curiosity. I had been on a movie set once. My friend Pauline from school had a friend who got a small part in some low-key television movie and invited us on a day tour as a treat. That movie set had been a busy place. There had been lots of people, cameras, monitors, food stalls, long rows of wires, and equipment everywhere. There was nothing here but a burning house, two cows, and some men. Were they actors? I gazed at them for longer this time and saw that each man was holding a type of stick or something in their hands.

This was just plain odd, but one thing I knew from growing up in the city was that if you thought it was trouble, it probably was trouble. I decided, movie set or no movie set, to run. I broke into a jog and, for want of a better direction, set off after the girl and woman. As I went by the house, and felt the heat coming from the crackling thatch, I saw a man lying prone on the ground. There was a rod with feathers at the end sticking out of his chest. This was no movie set.

In Memory of Dang,
With us for a short time, but the best of times

Prologue

6000 B.C.

I remembered how the old woman would sit on the log stool and poke continuously at the fire that my mother kept burning day and night. The hearth was located in the center of the big room in our house on hardened clay surrounded by a circle of stones. Grandmother was, it seemed to me at that young age, as eternal as the flame. She simply always was there. She was settled and quiet in front of the fire for most of the time, content to be with the rest of us, and left to dwell on what she alone knew ran through her mind. It was only on rare times, well into the night, that she sometimes livened up. Then, when the men had finished their talking of cattle and crops, when the youngest children had drifted asleep in their mother's arms and the family was hushed around the fire, would she talk. The story was always the same one with the same beginning and always about the same stranger.

"I remember the arrow," she would say. "How the flint head flashed in the sunlight as it struck down my father in front of the burning house. I remember the terrible fear and pain as my mother screamed out. And how the Wolf Man loomed up in front of me, axe in hand and ready to strike, when that wonderful boy, with his odd words and strange clothes, appeared as if from nowhere."

Chapter One

Present Day

"Henry, turn it off."

"Nearly finished, Dad."

"And we're nearly there. Turn it off now, please, or I'll take it for the rest of the afternoon."

I knew the threat was real enough, as he had done so before, and so reluctantly I switched off the game app. I slipped the phone into my jacket pocket and looked ahead at the road.

"Just relax," I said after a moment.

"I am relaxed."

"You don't seem relaxed."

"I am relaxed," he said slowly. "You know Grandad hates those phones."

"Grandad is living in the stone age."

"We're here now. Maybe you can leave it off, for me, and try to show some interest in what he's saying."

"Like you do?"

He said nothing, deliberately ignoring my remark, and turned off the main road. The car glided along the driveway up to the large ivy-covered house to stop in line with the front porch. Grandad lived on the far edge of the city where there were still some open fields and scattered patches of trees. He kept the gardens and exterior of the house in pristine condition, but the interior had not been changed or decorated in years.

"Out, and try to be good, just for the afternoon," Dad said, gathering up his coat and bag. "And when we get home, you can play your silly games for the rest of the night if you want."

"How long are we staying?" I asked as we walked to the door.

"Henry, I told you, we're staying for dinner. Let's have a nice family afternoon. I am asking you as a favor to me. Besides, it's not that bad. You used to love coming here when you were small, listening to Grandad's stories and looking at all his cool things."

"Dad, please, I was a kid then."

"But all those arrowheads and axes are still exciting, aren't they?"

"They were, when I was a kid. I'm not a child anymore. Anyways, he doesn't let me go near them."

"Because they're thousands of years old. They're valuable, I guess. He spent years at the university collecting them."

He pressed the doorbell and we waited in silence. I was not looking forward to this. An entire afternoon wasted doing nothing, basically.

A few moments later, the door was opened by Grandad, tall and slim, leaning on a walking stick.

"Well, my two boys, good to see you," he said with a smile.

I went forward and gave the older man a brief half-hearted hug, as was expected. He tapped me on the shoulder and was probably as relieved as me when I pulled away.

"Grandad, missed you."

"I am sure you did."

My dad and the older man shook hands.

"You're late," Grandad pointed out.

"The hospital called me in this morning. There was a problem with one of my patients and I had to sort it out first. Work is always...busy. You know how it is."

"Work, work, work," Grandad said, turning into the house. "That's all the younger generation does these days. You have all those gadgets and machines, and still you work all the time. Come in."

The two of them had settled down in the front room with

coffee to discuss what they always talked about—Grandad's health and his continued insistence on living alone in the house. My dad wanted him to sell the house and move into an apartment closer to us in the city, but Grandad always, politely, refused. I was sitting in a large antique chair beside an overgrown, almost wild, fern and was growing increasingly bored by the conversation. At my first planned and deliberate yawn, I was given the "nod" from my dad. That meant I was officially excused at least until dinner. After a few moments, I slipped out from the chair and left the room to roam the house.

As a child, I had spent hours in the house running from room to room or playing on the floor of Grandad's office, messing around with toys while he worked on his latest academic paper. The house had been huge and exciting back then, but now just seemed old-fashioned and borderline unkempt.

I found myself walking, almost without knowing, toward the old office on the ground floor. Reaching it, I pushed the door open and peered in. It was exactly the same as it had always been. The oak desk was piled high with papers, books, letterheads, and various odds and bits. The shelves were similarly cluttered and dusty.

My phone started to ring in my pocket and I was turning away from the door to answer it when I noticed the glass case on the wall behind the desk.

As the phone rang on, I glanced over my shoulder to make sure my dad had not crept up on me and then stepped into the room. I went around the desk to the glass case. I remembered, as Dad had mentioned in the car, it contained a number of stray finds from some of the many archaeological excavations Grandad had worked on all over the country.

The phone stopped ringing.

It was true what Dad had said, I used to love listening to what I thought then were thrilling tales from Grandad's time as an archaeologist. I would look with awe over his collection of ancient flint arrowheads, broken ceramic pieces, and pieces of animal bone he had inadvertently or on purpose forgotten to hand into the university.

As I looked down at the collection in the case, it now, however, seemed drab and uninteresting. But then I gave a short laugh for there, resting on the top shelf covered in dust, was the small arrowhead which, in a jolt I abruptly recalled, had so fascinated me as a child. It had been struck from a single piece of pure white flint except for a black jagged line, looking almost like a stylized lightning strike, running down its center. I wondered, then and there in the moment, what the arrowhead felt like to touch. As Dad had said, Grandad never allowed me to hold them when I was a child, saying they were too fragile. What he really meant, of course, was he did not trust me not to break them.

I reached up and pulled at the round handle on the front of the case. It was locked. I pulled again harder. To my surprise, the lock simply snapped away under my strength and the door to the glass case popped out. I had not meant to do that, had I? Either way, the glass case was now open. Slowly, inch by inch, I brought my hand up toward the arrowhead. My finger grazed the hard smooth surface.

I felt a punch against my shoulder as I slammed straight into something large. The impact and unexpected sting shook my whole body. What had happened? Had I slipped and somehow fallen against the desk? The object I had banged into was thrown forward, though, by the crash. It hit the ground, which I realized was not covered anymore in the wooden floorboards of Grandad's office, but tall brown grass.

Where was I exactly? Had I not just been in the house? I peered down at the object and saw it was covered in short hairs and now lay still. Had Grandad gotten a dog without telling anyone? After a moment, when my mind caught up with the reality of what my eyes were seeing, I saw in fact that it not an animal but a man who, for whatever reason, was dressed in a dog costume of some sort. Now that he was lying down, I could clearly see his form underneath the costume. He seemed to have stopped cold. To his right, I just then noticed, there was a large stick on fire implanted into the ground.

What was going on? The whole thing must, I thought, be part of a stage play that the man was acting in. The costumes and flaming stick all looked like they came from one of Shakespeare's plays, *King Lear* or one of them, that we had read in school over the years. I stepped around the man, more out of curiosity than for any sane reason, and saw that he had a gash of blood on his forehead. A very realistic bright berry red, I had to admit. There was a boulder protruding from the ground and it almost appeared as if he had fallen and hit his head on that. How, though, had I gone from Grandad's office into a play and, moreover, one that was set outdoors? Had I fallen out one of the windows into the garden? I needed to find out where I was first.

I looked up from the man to see a wooden house with its roof on fire, grey smoke drifting up into a pale blue sky, a short distance away. The house was standing in the middle of a large clearing surrounded by woodland. Perhaps it was not a play after all. Was I on a movie set instead? A girl appeared in front of me. Where had she come from? Had she been hiding in the grass? She was about my age with raven-colored hair cut short and stood up to my shoulder. She was also wearing a strange animal costume. She shouted something I did not understand. She must not speak English, I thought, so maybe she was from abroad. She was very pretty, I noticed. Again, the girl said something, quieter this time, and pointed away from me over my shoulder. I turned around and found another older woman standing there.

"Hello," I said.

Then, behind the older woman, where the ground sloped slightly downward, I saw what the girl was probably really pointing to. A line of men, five or six, likewise dressed in dog costumes, were slowly coming up the incline toward us. I watched them for a few moments. Was it just me or did they seem to be spreading out as they got nearer, as if, almost ridiculously I thought, they were attempting to circle around us. Who were these men?

Everything seemed wrong here. The girl said something once more and reached out to grab my hand to pull me toward her. I stumbled a foot or so in her direction but then remained there in a stunned sort of way trying to figure out what was going on. I just could not understand what she wanted, but I could see she was genuinely scared. She shook her head at me and, releasing me to take the hand of the older woman, they both ran toward the burning house. I watched them as they reached the house and veered off to one side to head for the tree line behind.

Why were they fleeing a movie set? I looked about me

again and saw, other than the men who were still getting closer all the while, there was now no one else near me. The only other structure I saw was a timber fence about twenty feet away with two shaggy brown cows who stared at the burning house with detached bovine curiosity. I had been on a movie set once. My friend Pauline from school had a friend who got a small part in some low-key television movie and invited us on a day tour as a treat. That movie set had been a busy place. There had been lots of people, cameras, monitors, food stalls, long rows of wires, and equipment everywhere. There was nothing here but a burning house, two cows, and some men. Were they actors? I gazed at them for longer this time and saw that each man was holding a type of stick or something in their hands.

This was just plain odd, but one thing I knew from growing up in the city was that if you thought it was trouble, it probably was trouble. I decided, movie set or no movie set, to run. I broke into a jog and, for want of a better direction, set off after the girl and woman. As I went by the house, and felt the heat coming from the crackling thatch, I saw a man lying prone on the ground. There was a rod with feathers at the end sticking out of his chest. This was no movie set.

Chapter Two

The Wolf Men attacked during the day while Yellow Face was still in the sky looking down. Such was the arrogance of the Wolf Men. They did not even hide their crime in the darkness.

I was by the river, collecting water for the night, with my mother. We were idly discussing how soon the heavily pregnant cow might give birth when I smelled the smoke coming through the trees. I knew in a moment something terrible was happening. I dropped the water jug and ran back along the path with my mother coming behind me. We broke into the clearing as the fire was spreading to cover the entire roof of our house. I saw my father there. He must have been inside the house and had come out, for he was standing right in front of the doorway. He was peering out through the smoke across the farm to see where the attack had come from. I spotted the archer, in the wheat field with his back to us, who had fired the burning arrows onto the roof.

The archer must have seen my father as well for he selected another arrow from his quiver and, not wasting time to light it from the torch struck into the ground beside him, pulled back on the bow.

I knew my father would not hear me over the noise of the fire so, instead, without even thinking about my actions, I set off running toward the archer. I was unarmed and he was twice my size, but I had to do something to help. I covered the ground between myself and the archer as he took aim. I was nearly there. All I had to do was to reach out and hit his arm to knock him off balance, but I was too late.

The archer let loose and I could only watch as the arrowhead flashed in the evening sunlight and a moment later hit my father in the chest. My mother followed its deadly progress too, for she let out a deep scream behind me as it struck.

The archer heard the scream, turned, and saw me nearly on top of him. He dropped the bow and reached for an axe he was carrying tucked in at his waist. He clearly meant to strike out at me, when, how can I describe it, a boy appeared in the wheat field and knocked the archer down. That was exactly how it was. The boy was not there and then he was. I came to a halt, unsure of what was happening and what to do next.

The boy moved around to look over the fallen archer. He must have then noticed me for the first time, for he stopped and stared at me intently. He was tall, young, not quite a man yet, and had a handsome look with hair, cut much longer than normal for a man, squashed down tight. He was also dressed in the oddest clothes I had ever seen, all straight and smooth with intense colors. He was gaping at me as if wondering what I was doing there. I had no idea who he was, where he had come from, or how he had gotten here. However, I did not have time to think about it.

I looked around and saw a line of Wolf Men coming up the hill to the house. The archer had been sent forward alone to set the fire, but these men were here to finish the task. They must have seen what had happened as well, the sudden attack on their man by the boy, for they were hanging back equally unsure of how to approach him.

"Behind you," I shouted at the boy.

He remained motionless.

"Behind you," I repeated, and pointed over his shoulder to the men.

He turned and gazed in their direction. He said something that I could not catch, but still did not move. We could not stay here. The Wolf Men would not remain surprised for very long. I reached out and pulled his arm, but he seemed rooted to the spot. Who was this boy? Maybe he could look after himself. He had, after all, just knocked out one of the Wolf Men single-handily. Besides, I had to take care of my mother.

"You should get away from here," I said quieter.

I let him go and took my mother's hand. Together, we ran. Whoever the boy was, he had given us enough time to get away. There was only one place to run to. The forest. As we went past the burning house, I saw my father on his back in front of the home he had built with his own hands and had been so proud of. He had now gone to join his ancestors. That was another thing I could not think about at this time.

We reached the river below the house and, without pausing, I pushed my mother straight into the water and jumped in after her. The river was only knee-high at the deepest point, but I must have slipped because I landed in the middle of the flowing water. The water engulfed me wholly, washing over my head. I got up through the force of the river and took a moment to get my footing. I heard splashing behind me and looked around to see, to my relief, not one of the Wolf Men but the boy. He reached out a hand toward me, which I grabbed, and together we headed for the far bank.

I knew the area around the farm far better than our attackers did. I had spent whole days wandering the forest near our home while my father cut wood for the cold winters. He had always warned me, though, not to go too far, for the forest was a dangerous place of wild animals and, of course, the Forest People. Now, we had no other choice but to head into its green-tangled embrace.

After the river, I found the small path that myself and my father used when entering the forest. We moved along the path until reaching an end clearing. Over the years, my father had slowly widened the open space as he cut down more and more of the encircling trees and stacked the wood in the center. A large boar rooting among the short grass was startled at our approach and skirted away. Were the Wolf Men following us, I wondered? They would have little difficulty tracking us as three people, without any attempt at concealment, would be easy to trail. We needed to put as much distance as possible between us and them. I was hoping, that even if they did venture in after us, that the farther in we went, leaving the path behind and going beyond the clearance where even I had not previously explored, they would grow afraid of the shadows and give up.

As we went on deeper into the trees, I could see that my mother was starting to falter. I pressed ahead nonetheless and the others followed. The terrain became more uneven and harder to cross, the ground full of fallen branches and thick knots of thorny undergrowth. It was impossible to judge where Yellow Face now sat in the sky as the wide tree canopy blocked out everything above us other than the shifting glimpses of greying sky and clouds.

As the trees around us seemed to grow taller at the approaching darkness, I knew we would need to stop soon. Alone in the forest with no food, water, or shelter, we had to find somewhere suitable to rest. We could not go back to the farm as undoubtedly the Wolf Men would leave a guard to watch for us. We pushed on a little farther until, taking in the state of my mother, I decided to stop.

I stood listening for any signs of pursuit, but I heard nothing other than the loud squish of the wind above me in the tree tops and the evening calls of the birds. I looked around where we had come to a halt and saw a fallen tree a short way off. It must have toppled over in the previous winter storms, leaving behind a huge hole in the ground blocked off on one side by a towering wall of the roots and compacted earth. It was perfect. I pulled my mother down into the hole and the boy followed. We lay there, panting, and my mother began crying softly. I crawled up to the edge of the hole and looked out. I could see or hear nothing other than the forest around us awaking to the night. Yellow Face was sleeping and her spouse, White Face, was waiting to appear to woo her in the dark sky as he did most nights. I slid down the bank and joined the other two.

"We need a fire," I said. "We will be fine here for the night, but we need warmth to dry our clothes. We can make a low fire here in the hollow, and it won't be visible through the trees."

My mother nodded but was already falling asleep where she lay. Hopefully, I thought as I set to work gathering the loose twigs and branches around me for the fire, even if they had dared follow us, the Wolf Men would not stay in the forest at night. After all, there were a lot more frightening things living in the forest than wolves.

I really began to worry when I saw there was no signal on my phone. I slid it open and was greeted by the regular smiling photo of my mum on holidays in Spain several years ago. My parents had met when they were both doing some volunteer medical work in Brazil. My dad said that my mum always loved traveling. That was the last holiday we had been on together. In fact, that was the last holiday ever. The signal bar showed nothing. I opened my apps and saw they had not been updated with the usual chit-chat and casual happenings since that morning. Across the fire, that somehow the girl had managed to get going out of a few twigs and crumbled leaves like something out of a survivor television show, she was staring at the phone in my hand.

"There's no signal," I pointed out more for something to say than expecting her to understand. "I don't suppose you have a phone on you by any chance?"

She said nothing.

"I didn't think so," I said.

She then stood, came over around the fire to me, and reached out to touch the phone with one finger.

"You want to have a look," I said, turning it out to face her.

She saw the photo of my mother, gasped, and actually scuttled back a foot or two.

"It's just a phone, look." I held up the display screen so we both could see it and flipped through some of the other photos.

"That's my dad," I said. "The café this morning, we always go there before going to see Grandad. That's what I had, a croissant and cappuccino. And that's Pauline, from school, well, don't mind that about her, that's nothing, just the car, the street, now that's Mick, he's a good friend."

She muttered something and reached out to the phone again. I let her hands wrap around the plastic cover, her fingers touching mine, and she pulled it over to herself. She tapped her finger on the screen a few times as I had done. She must have left the photo album and turned on the game I was playing earlier in the car because the phone let out a chirpy wail and she dropped it in fright. I laughed, not the smartest thing to do as she glared at me, and picked it up.

"I might just let it power itself down," I said, thinking it would be best to limit my usage as I had a feeling there probably was not much chance of charging it up any time soon. On the other hand, I did not want to turn it off completely just in case someone rang me.

The girl moved around the fire to the other woman. I settled down into the ground and pushed out my feet to the warmth. I was exhausted after all the excitement. What a day, what an odd day. I really wished I could get a connection so I could post a few pictures. They certainly would be a lot different from the typical everyday ones I usually posted. I still had no idea where I was or how I got here, but for the moment, in the hole by the fire, I reckoned I was safe enough. I looked across at the girl who was staring intently into the fire as if deliberately ignoring me. She and the older woman must surely be mother and daughter. And the man at the house? Her father maybe? My shoes were starting to dry off in the heat, and it was actually quite comfortable there. It reminded me of camping with my parents when I was a boy. I felt drowsy and thought, tomorrow, when it gets bright, I can find out exactly what was going on and get it all sorted.

Chapter Three

I was woken by the boy pulling at my foot. I slowly drew my foot back, not sure if I wanted him to touch me. I had fallen asleep with dreams of that smooth rock he possessed, which blazed with such color and was able to show tiny people. I simply could not begin to understand it. I guess, in my mind, I had decided to ignore the rock and everything else that was off about him until things were a little quieter and I had more time to think. I looked across at him. He was pointing up at a man who was squatting on the edge of the hole and staring down into our makeshift encampment.

At first, I startled up, thinking it was one of the Wolf Men who had found us. Then, seeing the face blackened with charcoal and the feathers protruding out from his hair, I relaxed. Even under his painted persona, I recognized Crow. He was a year or two older than me, but had become the leader of the Forest People at the beginning of last winter when his father had joined their ancestors. I knew him, as he and my own father had traded a number of times since then. The Forest People would barter fresh meat, fruits, and tree-medicine in return for flint pieces and cattle hides. I had talked to Crow whenever he came down to the farm and found him likeable if not a little aloof. I stood and could see there were a few more of the Forest People with him around the rim of the hole.

The Forest People were the original inhabitants of the land and still lived among the trees by hunting game and gathering the wild plants that grew there so abundantly. They had been here in the land all alone until my people, who cleared away patches of the ancient trees, broke the ground to grow their crops and built fences to keep their animals safe, had arrived from over the Wide Water. Now, we had to share the same land. For the most part, we stayed away from the deep interior of the forest where they lived, and they stayed away from our farms other than meeting occasionally to trade for mutually desired items.

Still, our presence was changing them. Along with their own words, of which I understood a little, the younger generation of Forest People, such as Crow, had learned to speak our words as well. My father had always been wary of their presence, but had respected them and tried to get along with them as best as possible. We had all heard stories, true or not I did not know, of Forest People emerging from the trees to strike at isolated farming settlements—burning the houses, killing the inhabitants, and taking the cattle for themselves. I had often wondered if they told similar stories about us—farmers coming to burn their settlements and steal their land away from them.

"Crow," I said, looking up at him.

"Wild Flower, you slept here all night?" he asked.

"Yes."

"We saw the smoke from your farm. Wolf Men?"

"They murdered my father."

"I am sorry to hear that. He was a good man." he nodded, and I could tell I was just confirming something he already knew. "They came into the forest afterward, following you, obviously."

"And what happened?" I asked.

"We warned them before, over and over, not to come here," he said, as if readying himself to confess some secret. "My father even went to talk to Wolf Killer personally at the River Settlement to tell him to keep his men away from us. And this time, they sent six armed men. I had to send them a clear signal or, next time, they would have sent even more."

"What did you do?" I pressed.

"I only wanted to scare them off. That was all. I told my archers to let off a few arrows over their heads. I never intended to hurt them."

"And?"

"One of my young men got a little excited and aimed directly for them. A man was hit in the shoulder and was bleeding a lot."

"Is he still alive?"

"No," Crow said. "He joined his ancestors in the night. They ran away and left him. We cared for him as best we could, but he still joined his ancestors. Before he left, though, he was muttering a bizarre story about the attack on your home. I thought at first that he had drunk some of that crazy apple brew your people love to drink. He said that a real-life breathing ancestor fell from the sky to attack a Wolf Man. I was curious, so I came to find you. Is that the ancestor?"

"Yes."

"He looks a little scrawny. Perhaps the ancestors of your people didn't have enough food?" His attempt at a joke meant he had acknowledged everything he thought I needed to know about the Wolf Men.

"I am not sure he is one of our ancestors," I said. "He speaks strange words. We cannot understand each other."

"His clothes are..."

"I know. There is more, believe me. I do not know who he is, but he did save us from a Wolf Man."

"And now, what will you do?"

"We'll head for the Lake Settlement, to my uncle," I said.

"And what about Wolf Killer?"

"I don't know."

"His men will be heading back to the River Settlement. One of the Wolf Men was killed here in the forest and the others who fled will lie. They will tell Wolf Killer that they fought bravely and that we attacked them without any cause. You have brought a lot of trouble with you, Wild Flower."

"We had nowhere else to go."

"Your father always treated us with respect, I appreciated that, but Wolf Killer will not forget this," he said.

"He's the one who attacked my farm and invaded your home."

"That doesn't matter. Wolf Killer is strong, and like all strong men, he cannot let an insult go unanswered."

"I am sorry, Crow, to bring this trouble to you. Help me get to the Lake Settlement, and I will talk to my uncle. Bring us through the forest and over the mountain, and then we are gone."

"Fine, I will help you if only to get you out of here. I will send a runner ahead to warn your uncle what was happened and tell him you are coming. Now, you are our guests in the forest. Let us eat, and afterward, we will bring you to the Lake Settlement."

I was not as fit as these guys. That was obvious. The hike was killing me while they had barely broken a sweat.

Before we set off, we had eaten breakfast. They handed around some red berries, a sort of nut paste served on a yellow leaf, and a type of lumpy, fruity baked bread. The food was different from what I was used to for breakfast. It was way too healthy and did not have enough sugar. It was like the homemade products for sale in an up-scale Farmer's Market. I had been starving by that time, though, so I ate whatever they gave me. I had to admit, it was fresh and tasted pretty good. A container of cold water, made from a part of some poor animal judging by the hairs still on it, was handed around. They all drank from it and no one seemed concerned about everyone sharing the same mouthpiece. I wiped it as best I could on my jacket and took a drink. I would have killed for a cup of coffee.

The girl from the farm yesterday and that odd fellow who had been staring down at us when I had woken up stopped talking after we climbed out of the hole, but I saw him watching her while she ate. And I mean *watching* her. He was definitely interested in her. What was with the black paint and all those feathers he was wearing? A bit dramatic, I reckoned. What was he meant to be, a bird?

There were two other lads, also dressed similarly, and a girl wearing the same attire except for a single white feather that was nearly lost among the black ones stuck into her hair. I did not know if the white feather meant anything particular for the group or she just wore it to stand out from the rest. I liked the touch, however.

After breakfast, they just stood up and started hiking through the woods. The girl from the farm, Farm Girl was a good name for her, and her mother followed and, only after a few steps, did she turn to make sure I was coming as well. To be honest, I had no idea where they were going or even if I was meant to go with them. I was still just standing there. She frowned and waved a hand for me to follow. I walked after them. What else could I do?

The Bird Guy, a good name for him as well, went ahead in front of the small group, leading us along narrow tracks which, I swear, were not even there until he stepped on to them.

Now, in the daylight, I could see that the forest around us was totally unlike the woods I had visited when younger with my dad and mum. There were no neat gravel footpaths and signposts pointing out the visitor café. This forest was not managed in any way. It was wild and free. All types of trees grew out and twisted upward, intertwining with one another as they fought to reach the sunlight above. Most of the jumbled forest floor was cast into permanent lime-tinged semi-darkness. I found the environment disorientating. It was impossible to tell the time or the passing of the day, and I had no idea how long we were walking or what direction we were going. Most of the way, we were going uphill, that was as much as I got.

Everyone else in the group seemed to move with ease over the terrain, but I fell behind constantly and found the going hard. I did sports at school, but this was a whole different ball game. This was really tough. I even wondered if they had slowed down their normal pace, or maybe they had taken an easier route for me and the mother. Well, probably for me mostly. The mother stumbled once or twice, but the girl was there to help her. I was clearly the weakest of the bunch. A few times one of the other guys dressed up like birds pointed at me following behind and started arguing with Bird Guy until a few sharp words from Bird Guy shut him up.

We went on for most of the day and only stopped for the night much later. They produced rolls of leaves, which contained similar types of foods as the breakfast. No wonder they were so fit if this was all they ate. This time, I drank from the container without any problem. They built a fire, a large one this time, and we sat around it. As I fell asleep, I saw Farm Girl and Bird Guy opposite me talking in hushed tones.

In the morning, we set off again. We had been traveling uphill all the time and the higher we went, the trees began to clear. At one point, I decided to stop and try the phone one more time, thinking that maybe there might be a connection up so high. I sat on a boulder, pulled out the phone, and checked it for a signal, but, as I had been kind of expecting, there was nothing.

I looked up from the phone and out through the thinning trees over the view below. It was simply incredible. The forest, deep and emerald, rolled away down the side of the mountain we were climbing. Only toward the foot of the mountain, as the ground leveled off, could I see a small break in the tree covering where a thin column of smoke hung in the air. I guessed it was the remains of the burning house from the other day. In the far distance, I could see a line of silver as a river coiled through the landscape. Where was I exactly? There was no forest like this at home anymore. Somehow, I had been taken from Grandad's house and brought some-where else. Where though? My best guess was South Ameri-ca. I had never been to the Amazon, but I had seen it on tele-vision and online. It was the only place in the world I knew of that still had huge intact forest cover like this.

The guy, the one giving trouble to Bird Guy yesterday about me slowing them down, must have crept up, because he suddenly stepped out in front of me and punched me on the shoulder. Maybe that was his way of saying "get a move on," or that was how they said "hello" but I seriously doubted it. I stood up slowly so he was less than a foot away from me and stared at him. He was not so big when I was next to him. Maybe he realized that because he glanced down, breaking eye contact, just for a moment, before looking at me once more.

"Don't do that," I said.

He said something in their language. What did they speak in South America—Spanish or Portuguese, wasn't it? It did not sound like any of those languages. I may not have un-derstood the words, but I got the meaning. He was trying to boss me around. What had Dad always said—don't go look-ing for a fight, get out of any trouble you can without fighting, but don't let anyone boss you around either. The guy said something again, but I kept my cool.

After a moment, he snorted in disgust and walked away. I watched him go and turned to see the rest of the group ob-serving our confrontation from farther up. Bird Guy nodded down at me in apparent approval. I felt as if I had passed some test without even knowing I was taking it.

As I climbed up to the rest of the group, the White Feather Girl murmured something, flicking her head toward the guy I had stood off with. I had no idea what she was saying but, yeah, I could only agree that he was a complete idiot.

We moved on for the rest of the day. I found it a little easier going now that we had broken out from the forest cover. Eventually, we reached the crest of the mountain, climbed over the windy summit that was barren except for a pile of stones on the scrubby growth, and moved down to the woods on the other side. As we began our descent, with still only a few trees here and there, I could finally see our destination. Below us, at the base of the mountain, the forest came to a sudden stop. The trees formed a clearly manmade edge around a cluster of several houses and smaller huts, some of which were emitting trails of smoke, amid criss-crossing paths and stretches of outlying fields. On the other side of the settlement, there was a good-sized lake, which I guessed must have been fed by a number of streams coming off the mountain. The lake in turn emptied into a river that ran through a series of low hills and off into the distance. From up here, I could hear someone shouting and a dog barking. Seeing the settlement below us, it was then that I knew where and, perhaps more shocking, *when* I was.

Chapter Four

My uncle was not a coward. I had heard the stories of his youthful bravery from my own father many times before, but I could see immediately that he was now afraid. He was frightened of my presence here and what it could mean for him. I could see his fear in the way he looked at me as we finally came down into the Lake Settlement.

He walked forward and raised his arm in greeting.

I lifted his hand and touched the back of the fingers to my forehead in a show of traditional respect, as a good niece should do, but I kept my eyes open. The Lake Settlement was where I was born and where I had spent my first early years, so I had a right to return whenever I wished. My ancestors were buried in the Stone House on the nearby hill. My uncle may not have wanted me here, but he could not stop me returning.

Crow and his Forest People kept close to me. Relationships between the Forest and Lake Peoples were cordial, but only just about. The Lake People had little reason to trade with the Forest People, as the lake with its plentiful supply of fish and their farms provided almost everything they needed. Instead, the Lake People frequently whispered accusations of stealing against the Forest People anytime anything went missing. Still, though, they feared them as well, wondering if they were being watched unseen from the tree line or if an arrow could come slipping someday from the leafy shade.

"The messenger arrived yesterday from the Forest People," my uncle said once our formal greetings were completed. "I grieve for my poor brother."

"He is with our ancestors now."

"And how is your mother coping?"

"She has not said a word since the attack."

"Give her time to mourn. Your father was a good man,

but I told him not to go. I told him that there was always a place here for him even after I became leader. I did not want him to leave, but he insisted. He had seen the good land on the other side of the mountain and wanted to break the ground for his family, that's what he said."

I had heard a different story from my mother. That my uncle and father had been very close as boys but had drifted apart as they grew older. Over time, their distance had turned into open rivalry as they competed against each other for standing in the settlement. It had always been assumed somehow that one of them would become leader once the last leader, Broken Tree, died.

When that happened, my uncle had been shrewder and faster in maneuvering himself into a position of power. He had promised continuity with the past to those in the settle-ment who were afraid of change. Once in power, though, he became worried that my father's presence in the settlement would undermine his own. He knew that some people had secretly wanted my father, who was pushing for change in how the settlement was operated, to fill the positon. Of course, there was nothing he could do in public, in front of other people, but in private he had spread false rumors about my father, blaming him when cattle got sick or crops were destroyed by drought or heavy rain. This went on until my father could stand it no longer and decided on leaving in order to be free from the lies.

"A good farmer always needs good land." I said.

"Perhaps, is that the ancestor?" my uncle asked, gestur-ing to where the boy was standing looking around him.

"Yes."

"He doesn't look like much. I thought he would be...taller somehow."

"Who can tell what an ancestor would look like?" I said.

"True," my uncle said slowly, as if not believing my words. "Now, though, you must rest. You have had a long journey. You and your mother will stay with me. I have pre-pared a separate hut for the ancestor. Rest now and we will hold an assembly in the morning."

"I am not tired," I said. "It would be better to have the assembly now. Otherwise, people will spend the night afraid of what I am going to say. It is better they hear it before they sleep."

My uncle thought over my request and then nodded.

"And with your permission, I would ask that Crow also stays."

"Why?" my uncle asked suspiciously.

"He brought us over the mountain. He fed me and my mother. The least we can do is offer them one night's hospitality in return. Besides, it will reflect well on you if you show them the proper welcome."

My uncle glanced over the band of Forest People, trying to decide if their small numbers meant they were a threat or not, and nodded again. I was glad of it because I did not trust him. I was hoping Crow's presence would provide me with some protection if needed.

My uncle's house was the largest in the settlement. The interior was reached by going through an internal porch formed by the side of the house and a timber wattle frame held up by two posts at either end. This opened out onto a big room which was used as the main living area where the inhabitants ate and slept around a stone-lined hearth. At the end of the room there was another partition across the width of the house with a narrow middle doorway, currently curtained off, leading to the back rooms used for work and storage. It was the same house I had played in as a child, the same house my father had grown up in, and the same house his father had built and died in. It was a strong home formed not only by the stout timber walls and great rafters spanning the roof, but by the generations of tough farmers who had lived therein.

I went to sit by the fire as I watched the Lake People troop in and take up places around the room, sitting on the furniture or the ground. Some were staring openly at the strangers in their midst. It was odd enough that a band of Forest People sat in the leader's house, but also a living ancestor. The boy himself seemed quiet, tired perhaps, and sat apart with a small ceramic bowl, nothing more than a drinking cup, which he turned over and over in his hand as if only seeing one for the first time. My uncle waited until most of the people had arrived until he stood and spread out his hands for quiet. The crowd fell silent other than the odd giggle or squeal of a child who was rebuked and hushed by their mother.

"This is a sad time for us," my uncle said. "One of our own has been killed, my own brother. By now, you will all have heard what the messenger from the Forest People said on the matter. My niece is here, so let us hear her version."

I stood, and for the first time, I recounted the events of the past few days. I told how one of the Wolf Men had used flaming arrows to set the roof of the house alight. How my father rushed out as we returned from the river. I told how I had personally seen the Wolf Man bring the arrow to bear on my father and then let it fly. How the same archer would have subsequently used his axe on me had it not been for the arrival of the ancestor who knocked down the archer with a single blow. Lastly, I told how we ran, through the river and into the forest, to escape with our lives.

As I talked, I suddenly felt the great loss that my mother and I had suffered. Not only was our home, our farm, and our cattle gone, but more importantly we had lost my father. My caring and resilient father who always had time to stop in his never-ending chores around the farm to spend time with me. As I talked of the day of the attack, I felt the tears swelling within my heart, but pushed the crying deep down. I needed to remain coherent in front of the Lake People so they could hear clearly what happened.

After I had finished, the entire room was silent. The children stared open-mouthed at my story while the adults were somber, thinking perhaps of their own timber homes, which would burn as easily as mine did. I hoped that by telling the story as it was, by not forgetting any detail or adding in any false word, it would make my uncle and the whole settlement realize what my mother and I had suffered. And I had to make them understand who was to blame—Wolf Killer.

I waited for a response from my uncle, but he remained sitting and did not even look at me. Instead, out stepped First Calf, a man so close to my uncle that my father had often joked he was the true leader of the Lake Settlement. I knew then that my uncle was not going to take on the responsibilities due toward my father. In sending First Calf to speak for him, he showed that he was looking for a way out of his duties.

"Wild Flower, our hearts are heavy with never-ending sorrow for your loss," First Calf said with pronounced formality. "And for your father to meet such an end, fighting to protect his land and his family, was both glorious and awful. His death was a terrible tragedy. May he now be happy in the Stone House of his ancestors."

"Thank you, First Calf, for your words." I decided to press the main point immediately rather than give him time to evade the question. "But what will the Lake Settlement do in response?"

"Calm down, Wild Flower, you have suffered a great tragedy. You are tired and emotional."

"I am neither, but I am a little confused. You keep speaking of a tragedy. My father's death was not a tragedy. We were attacked for no reason by the Wolf Men. My father was murdered by Wolf Killer."

"Well, let's not get ahead of ourselves. We do not know exactly what happened. We only have your account of the story, and even if the Wolf Men were there, we cannot then inevitably lay the blame on Wolf Killer. We do not know that he was personally involved. Was Wolf Killer there? Do you know what he looks like?"

"No, how would I? I have never met him."

"Exactly," First Calf said. "And, to be honest, how do we really even know that the men there were Wolf Men? They were dressed in wolves' clothing, true, but anyone can put on an animal fur and claim to be a Wolf Man. We simply don't know. The men could have come from anywhere, not necessarily from the River Settlement."

I could see that the strategy of my uncle, speaking through First Calf, was to cast doubt on my story. This would allow him to then claim that there was no way of knowing for certain if it really was the Wolf Men who attacked my farm. Therefore, it would be imprudent, if not outright foolish, to blame them. My uncle's plan of action was to ignore the problem. I could not let that happen as that would put everyone, including me, my mother, and the entire settlement, in danger.

"And as for this boy you say saved you." First Calf waved a hand toward the ancestor. "Well, we have no idea where he came from either. We have no idea what sort of company your father kept. Possibly he was merely hiding in the house when the attack happened and he came running out. In all the smoke, you could not have seen what really happened. Isn't that true, Wild Flower?"

"I never saw the boy until that day. And how do you explain his clothes?"

"That is easy. There are many other peoples out there with their own customs and odd ways that we know nothing about. Perhaps he is simply a trader from far away who had stopped at your farm when you and your mother were down by the river. After your father invited him in, the attack took place. That would explain his strange clothes and words, and it would make sense. Surely one of our ancestors would know our words?"

Some of the people listening murmured their approval at this claim. As First Calf opened his hands to the crowd, soaking up their support, I looked around the room. I sensed, as with my uncle, that most of the settlement was happy for First Calf to speak so, to throw shadows onto my story. Then, they too could avoid thinking about the death of my father, one of their own, and in doing so avoid having to worry about the attack on my farm. These people were, I realized, terrified of Wolf Killer and the Wolf Men. They were terrified that what had happened to my farm could happen here as well. In their fear, they were willing to hold onto to any irrational argument that seemed to offer them a safe way out. I knew, for the moment at least, with First Calf leading them on, that I had lost the argument even before I had stood to speak.

"Tell me, First Calf," I said. "Do you think that the mountain between you and Wolf Killer will save you?"

"Do not show disrespect to me," First Calf snapped. "Remember that you and your mother are without a home now."

"This is our home. Don't you ever forget that," I said. "Do you think you can make this problem go away by your clever words? The Wolf People are becoming stronger every year. Like a vine around the tree. Their power seeps over the land grasping at everything it touches. The attack on my farm shows that Wolf Killer is now looking this way, toward the Lake Settlement. So, if you think you safe here, you are wrong. My father thought we were safe, but still the Wolf Men came."

"Your father was a fool to leave the Lake Settlement in the first place," First Calf said.

"Perhaps," I said, looking directly at First Calf. "He did not like the smell of rotting fish here."

"Careful, Wild Flower, tread carefully," my uncle spoke for the first time. "Even if what you say is true, if you are right that Wolf Killer attacked your farm and that, somehow, that is a prelude to an attack here, that Wolf Killer wants to now expand his control over the mountain, what can we do? The Lake Settlement is small compared to the River Settlement. What can we do? We cannot stop Wolf Killer on our own. It is better for us to stay quiet and not draw his attention here."

"What you say is true, on our own we can do little, but there must be others who fear Wolf Killer. We sit on only one side of his domain. There must be other settlements and other peoples that would join a fight against him. And farther down our river, what of the settlements there? Perhaps they have heard of Wolf Killer and dread his approach. We used to travel and trade with the other settlements down the river before we turned back in on ourselves. What the Lake People said back then used to matter. We can send canoes to reestablish contact with the other settlements. And even the Forest People have a reason to join us now against him."

"I have heard rumors," my uncle said, glancing toward Crow's band, "that some of the Forest People have given up their old ways and joined with Wolf Killer."

I saw Crow grow annoyed at that accusation and start to stand. I shook my head at him. He paused, looking at the people around him who were edgy and frightened. They were looking for someone to blame for their troubles. Any harsh word from him could easily make them turn on his band. He regained his composure and sat down again.

"I am sure that some from every people have gone to join Wolf Killer. Power always attracts stray dogs. He does not control the whole land, though, not yet. Surely there are enough free settlements still left to unite against him."

"Perhaps there are," my uncle said. "But how will they come together? Who would raise their head first to be torn down by the wolf?"

"And so we do nothing," I said. "Instead, Wolf Killer will take each settlement and people one by one. With each conquest, his strength grows until we are all swallowed up and all the land is his. We will not be free. There will be no Lake People or any other free people, only Wolf People covering the whole land."

Some of the crowd around me openly grumbled at this last notion and a few turned to talk to their neighbors. I had obviously hit a sore point. If we were all to become Wolf People, that would mean our own ancestors would no longer recognize us when we traveled through the Grey Mist to join them. They would not then allow us to enter the Stone House of the Lake Settlement. Instead, we would have to reside in the Stone House of the Wolf People with ancestors we did not know. My uncle looked around and saw I had struck home an arrow. Feeling perhaps that the argument was suddenly turning against him and that he was in danger of losing control of the situation, he held up his hand for quiet.

"Dear niece, I can see that you are tired. We have had enough talk for today. We will meet again in the morning and discuss what we should do. Tonight, we must rest."

Chapter Five

It was the phone that saved me. Funny, all the complaining my dad did about the amount of time I spent on it, and it saved my life. The alarm beeped and I turned over absent-mindedly on the covering of bedding straw overlying the hard floor to flick it off. As I did, I saw a reminder, timed for when I should have been getting up for school, that it was Dad's birthday in a week and I needed to get him a present. I looked up from the phone, wondering what he would like, and saw the flint blade coming from the darkness toward me in the dim screen light.

What took hold of me? Was it instinct? Was it fear? I did not know. I just reacted. I dropped the phone, rolled across the floor, and struck out hard with my foot. I must have hit my attacker, because I heard a groan and saw a shape in the gloom fall back. I scrambled up onto my feet just in time as my attacker recovered and lunged at me again. I suddenly felt a red anger take hold of me. I was alone among strangers, abandoned in a place with no friends or family and, to be honest, I was starting to have caffeine, sugar, and online withdrawals. I was, to my surprise, even feeling a little homesick and starting to miss my dad. I was tired of having no control over my situation, and now, somebody was actually trying to kill me. Give me a break.

I half-turned to one side so the blade swished past me. As the attacker was now stretched out with the blade at full arm's length, I was able to come back in and punch him hard in the ribs where he was exposed. The groan was louder this time, but still he tried to bring the blade around for another attempt. I hit him again, harder in the jaw, and down he went to the floor. I stood over the now out cold figure. I felt the adrenaline flow through my body. I felt powerful. I felt awesome. I had not been in a fight since I was ten years old, with Mick who was now ironically my best friend, and yet I had just managed to knock out an assassin. Better than any video game.

I found the phone on the floor and shone the screen light onto the silent form. It was the same lad who had tried to push me around up on the mountain. Had he returned to make his point? Maybe it was a cultural thing, not trusting the stranger and wanting to get rid of him? What, it struck me, if he was not alone? The Bird Guy and some others had been with him after all, even the White Feather Girl, although I would like to think she was not involved.

I needed to get out into the open to deal better with the threat. Thinking that a weapon might be useful, I picked up the fallen flint blade by the handle, stepped over the lad who was starting to stir a little, and went out through the hut door. The sun was rising on the far mountain, but the settlement was still wrapped in the night. In front of me a dog, startled by my sudden appearance, starting yelping in my direction.

I heard a voice shouting somewhere and, now with the rush of the fight evaporating, decided it might be best to get away from the settlement altogether. Get away from these people who were trying to kill me. I set off at a steady pace past the sleeping houses, the animal pens with murmuring cattle, and the outer fields of swaying grain down to the lake.

The water was flat and still in the morning air. I slowed down and walked round the lake until coming to the river. I followed the calming water for a while. To the right, I saw the low hills I had spotted from atop the mountain. I made for the side of the nearest hill, which was covered by a small patch of woodland. Out of the entire surrounding area, those trees alone had not been cut down for fuel or timber supplies. They offered a place to hide. I only stopped when I reached the welcome cover of the trees. I rested with one hand on a branch to catch my breath. I heard distant shouts coming from the direction of the settlement and wondered if they were now looking for me.

I wanted some peace and quiet so I could think. I walked away from the edge of the woods deeper into its center. After only a minute or two, I came to an inner clearing in the trees, which contained a large mound of green grass ringed by a single line of white stones around its base. There was an opening into the mound directly facing me formed by two huge flat rocks, which had been placed well into the side of the mound. In front of the mound entrance, a woman, tightly wrapped against the morning air, was hunched over a small fire. The woman, with red hair, beautiful eyes, and a warm face smiled up at me almost as if she had been expecting me.

I went forward and, at her signal, sat on a log stump opposite her.

She seemed completely undisturbed by my arrival at her camp so early in the morning. She picked up a stone hollowed basin containing water and rested it on two side rocks over the fire.

I laughed aloud. What my grandad would have given to be sitting here with me. He would have been so excited and would have stared at everything. Though, I was almost certain the first thing he would have done was walk to the mound entrance and look inside. I knew, even without going there myself, he would have seen a cramped interior passageway, lined with similar large stones as the entrance pillars, which probably continued on through the length of the mound with one or more side-chambers branching off. I knew all this with such definite certainty from listening to Grandad's talks over the years and even flipping through the odd academic book when I was bored on yet another Sunday afternoon visit. He would have been proud, and perhaps a little surprised, that I learned something so useful in his company.

As a result of this second-hand knowledge, I recognized exactly what the structure was. It was a tomb, because I knew exactly where, or rather when, I was—the Neolithic period. That era in human history when agriculture first emerged and spread over centuries throughout the globe. When mankind moved from a hunter-gatherer lifestyle, like the existence evidently still lived by the people we had met in the forest, to one based around more or less permanent settlements. When people used stone to make tools as the use of metals had not been discovered yet. When people first grew crops and raised animals such as cattle, sheep, and pigs. I was in the time in our history when land became the most valuable resource in the world, when the population expanded and society became significantly more complex. It was also a time when the first elite leaders appeared and sought to control society for their own ends.

I first had an inkling where and when I was after seeing the settlement by the lake yesterday from the mountain top. Strange as it sounded, I had been there before. Or rather, I was going to go there in the future. I had gone to the site with my grandad a long time ago, when I was still young and interested. It was after he and his team had finished an excavation of one of the house structures and they were wrapping up the dig for the winter season. By that time, the place was a windswept uninhabited patch of open grass, although the lake and river were still there. As far as I was aware, the settlement was now a local curiosity for the odd tourist willing to travel down the small country roads to find it. At least I now knew where and when I was. The real question was— how did I get back home?

The woman, having decided that the water was hot enough, took the stone basin off the fire using a thick pad of leather so as not to burn her hands. She poured the water into a small, circular ceramic bowl she had left nearby. She took a stick and swirled the contents of the bowl around and then handed it over to me.

I held it, relishing the heat, while she made drinking motions with her hands. I brought the bowl up and smelled the contents. It reminded me of tea and honey. I took a small sip and grinned with the sweet taste. I had not had a single piece of chocolate or a biscuit in days. I took another longer gulp and finished the drink. I handed the bowl back to her.

She took it, smiled, and then nodded toward the tomb entrance. It was peculiar, but the tea seemed to drift through me, leaving me a little lightheaded. She nodded again at the entrance, clearly expecting me to go into the tomb.

I kind of wanted to do what she asked if only because she was so attractive and I figured that if the offer was there, maybe I should go in. To see what another person had not seen in thousands of years.

I stood, went over to the mound entrance, and bent over to look in. It was dark inside. I got down on my hands and knees and crawled forward, past the two looming entrance stones, into the short passageway beyond. The cold rock pressed against me on either side until I came to the larger inner chamber, which spread out around me. Despite the extra room, I was still barely able to stand and had to remain half bent over. With the light from the entrance coming in behind me, I could just make out the size and shape of the tomb interior.

It seemed much larger inside than the mound outside. The air was warm and tasted of smoke, as if a fire had been lit in there earlier and the after-effects still lingered. I felt a little dizzy in the confined area and sat down. I landed on something hard. It shifted underneath me and I heard a loud crunch. I reached down and pulled up a long fragment of a bone. Human or animal, I had no way of knowing. I hoped it was not human, because I think I just broke it. I looked up and saw a large compact circular swirl carved into the stone directly in front of me. The moving path from the outside into the inner point of the swirl was marked in red. I wondered if it was paint or blood.

I was not sure if it was the early morning, the fight, the flight from the settlement, or something in the tomb lady's warm tea, but suddenly, I felt dog-tired. My eyes drooped, and I decided to lay out flat on the earthen floor and bones. I needed to close my eyes, just for a moment. I needed to sleep, just for a short while. When I awoke, I would be rested and refreshed. Then I could come up with some sort of plan for getting home. After all, if I had been able to travel here, then there had to be a way to get home again.

It was crazy that I was here. How was it even possible? As I slumbered, I tried to remember some of the theories I had read about online or seen in science fiction television shows regarding events like this but could not come up with any firm notions.

A hand gripped my foot and, in fright, I looked up. I was surprised to see Grandad there. It was a younger, hazier version of the real man I knew at home but still recognizable as him. He had crawled into the tomb after me and was beaming at everything around him.

"Remarkable, Henry, just astounding. Have you noticed the ritualized deposition of bones? And did you see that the tomb is left open? It has not been sealed off. That could suggest it was used on a continuing basis, not just built and closed off for one event. These remains must be from the local settlement. These must be their ancestors. It is like a mirror reflection of the settlement by the lake, a home for the dead to live in."

"Grandad," I said, confused. "How did you get here?"

"How do you think?"

"You touched the arrowhead?"

"If that's how you got here, it could work for me."

"How is Dad?"

"I don't know."

"I want to get back home, but how, how can I get back?"

"It's your dream, Henry, you tell me."

"I have no idea."

"Think, you're intelligent enough to figure it out."

"Well, I guess, if the arrowhead got me here in the first place, then maybe it can get me back home. If touching the arrowhead in your office brought me here, then maybe I just need to touch it to get home again."

"Sounds plausible to me."

"But it still doesn't explain how all this is happening."

"Why do you think?"

"Are you just going to ask a load of questions or answer anything?"

"Like I said, Henry, it's your dream. You brought me here as a mouthpiece for your mind because I'm the most balanced, logical person you know. I'm not sure if I should be insulted or happy about that. What do you think?"

"Well," I said. "The arrowhead is important. That would make sense. And somehow it connects the two different worlds."

"The real question then is, why is it important?"

"Here, at least, it was the arrow that killed that poor girl's father at the burning house. She was so utterly focused on it, the arrow that ended her father's life, an arrow that she was completely emotionally invested in. She wanted it to miss, but it didn't."

"And?"

"And it's the same arrowhead I have known since I was young. I had forgotten about it until I saw it again in your house. It was the arrowhead you would never let me touch as a child. It..."

"Yes," he prompted.

"It almost represented my entire childhood, being told continually what to do and what I could not do. And how much harder it got after Mum's death, when it was just me and Dad. So, I was also emotionally attached to it, like the girl. I just didn't know it until now."

"So, the one artefact was the focus of two very different people across the spectrum of time." Grandad reached out and idly traced a finger over the engraved swirl. "The beginning and the end in one."

"Can I do it?" I asked.

"Find the arrowhead and get home?"

"Yes."

"That's up to you. Your dad raised you well, to be clever, quick, and strong. The rest is up to you."

"Tell me, Grandad. Did you know about the arrowhead? Is that why you never let me go near it?" I asked.

He said nothing, but smiled. My eyes opened and I was alone. Grandad was safe at home, and I was in a tomb with the dead. I pulled myself up from the floor of bones, turned around, and made my way out.

By this time, the sun was up and it took a moment to adjust to the bright sunshine.

Farm Girl was there talking with the tomb lady.

I did not know how she found me, but I was grateful she was there. Perhaps I was not as alone as I had thought. On seeing me, she pushed past the tomb lady and rushed over. I thought for a brief moment she was going to kiss me, but she pulled up short, as if stopping herself from doing that very thing. Instead, she clutched my shoulders with both hands.

I smiled at her. I knew what I had to now do. I had to return to the burning house and retrieve the arrowhead.

Chapter Six

The whole settlement had come alive with the morning events. One of the old men had gone out to investigate why his dog was barking and had seen a limping man leave the hut where the ancestor had slept. The man had glared at the old man as he went by, but did not approach as the growling dog had taken up a defensive positon in front of his master. The old man recognized him as one of the Forest People who had come down with my group. He started to shout, raising the alarm, but by the time anyone else appeared, the limping man was gone.

Arriving quickly on the scene, Crow spotted me and pushed through the small crowd who had come out to see what the fuss was all about. I noted, approvingly, that while some of the Lake People were still sleepy and rubbing their eyes, others were carrying weapons and were fully alert as if expecting Wolf Killer had already arrived. I wondered if may-be some of these people were a little more aware of the situation than my uncle seemed to be. If so, there might be hope for them after all.

"They are saying it was one of yours," I said to Crow. "Who?"

"Who do you think? The idiot Boar is missing, as stupid as his namesake. Let's see what happened."

Crow and I went into the hut where the ancestor had slept and he scrutinized the ground for a few moments, read-ing the mess of footprints on the earthen floor.

"He was attacked while he slept," he said. "He managed to get up out of the bedding and defend himself. You can see here, the two men stood opposite each other and fought. Boar probably had a knife as he tried to get close to the an-cestor, but there is no blood so he must have defended him-self well enough. He's pretty tough for a scrawny one."

"Why would Boar do it? He was hardly still upset over the incident on the mountain?"

"I don't know. I really don't."

"He could be working for Wolf Killer," I said to point out the obvious.

"Maybe. We will find him, don't worry about that, but first I have to get my people out of here. Your uncle will turn against us pretty quick after this."

"Fine. I have to find the boy, though."

I was able to track him without any problem up to the Stone House. He seemed to have no ability whatsoever to cover his footpaths like my father had taught me. I would make sure he was all right before settling the inevitable commotion that would now occur between the Lake People and the Forest People. I could not let this incident damage the relationship between us at this critical time. The shaman woman was waiting outside the Stone House.

"He's in there," she said.

"We have to get him out."

"No," she said firmly. "He has gone in alone and he must come out alone."

"He could be injured."

"He isn't. He is traveling through the Grey Mist to the ancestors. Don't go in, Wild Flower. It is up to him to see what he sees in there. He won't thank you if you disturb him."

I wanted to go in, but I knew she was right. We then waited for an age before, finally, the boy appeared and crawled out from the Stone House. He seemed a little dazed as he exited. I pushed past the shaman woman to greet him. I nearly embraced him, but at the last moment pulled myself up short. After all, I did not know him and feasibly he might have been already tied to some other woman. Although still young, he was old enough to be married. Nevertheless, I was pleased to see him alive and well. It seemed the two of us had been through a lot together and, even if he was already taken, I felt we should look out for each other if nothing else.

He seemed fine after a few moments out in the sunshine. He regained his composure and began talking quickly in those funny sounding words of his. He also kept making a gesture of holding up one clenched hand in front of himself and dragging his other hand back horizontally at his head level. It took a moment until I realized he was making the same motions as an archer would when pulling on an arrow in a bow.

I thought maybe he was referring to the attack on him that morning. That could not be right, though. None of the Forest People had brought their hunting bows with them. I nodded at him, and satisfied I had at least understood his first point, he pointed to the far mountain beyond the settlement. He was saying something I could not grasp. He kept repeating the same sounds over and over. He was smiling at me, waiting for me to get his meaning, but I simply could not understand what he was trying to say.

Finally, latching onto to my lack of comprehension, he knelt down in the dry dirt in front of the Stone House. He picked up a charcoal-ended stick from the shaman's fire and drew the outlines of what looked like a crude arrow on the ground between us.

The shaman woman grew very excited when he began drawing and almost pushed me out of the way to see what the picture was. The ancestor pointed several times at the head of the arrow. Then underneath the arrow he drew three short vertical straight lines, a small circle atop each line, slashed another line through the top of the vertical lines and then two lines slanting out from the bottom. He pointed at the smallest one of these line drawings and toward me, then at the largest of the drawings and lastly at the arrow.

I still had no idea what he was attempting to convey so, in order to get a better viewpoint from his perspective, I walked around him and laid a hand on his shoulder to look down at the drawing. At first, it still looked like a mass of lines and circles, but then I inhaled a short breath as, in a moment, the drawings seemed to converge into an obvious pattern and stand out against the brown earth. I saw what it was. He had drawn my family. I pulled back in shock. The shaman woman raced around to my positon and gave a small cry when she saw what he had done. My people often found expression in art. An imaginative art born of an inner mind, often seen by the shamans when in their trances, depicted as swirls, lines, and other such shapes. This, though, drawing my family so close to the Stone House, seemed wrong in some way. After all, both my mother and I were still alive. It was inauspicious to place us here in the home of the dead.

He gestured toward the small figure, obviously representing me, next to the large figure and to the top of the arrow.

If I was the small figure, I guessed the large figure must be my father. And the head of the arrow could only be the arrowhead that had struck him and brought him down. The boy pointed once more at the arrowhead, the figure of my dead father, and to the mountain.

I then realized what he wanted. He wanted to return to the farm for the arrowhead that had killed my father. Why? Was the arrowhead important somehow? Had he seen a vision in the Stone House? I did not understand, but there seemed to be lot going on that defied any practical explanation. I nodded at him.

Satisfied I had understood what he was trying to say, the boy stood and walked in the direction of the settlement. I brought up my foot and rubbed it across the figures, making them return to the dirt.

The shaman woman grabbed my arm as if to stop me, but it was too late. My family was gone.

I set off after the boy.

As I had reckoned, when we reached the settlement, there was trouble brewing between the Forest and Lake Peoples. The door of the hut where the Forest People had stayed was guarded by the girl with them. She kept a hand on a sheeted flint knife as a warning to the people that had gathered nearby, muttering among themselves. My uncle saw me arrive and walked over.

"I told you the Forest People could not be trusted. You would not listen."

"It was one man among them. Did the rest help him? No, they didn't. Otherwise they could have killed the ancestor on the way here, but a single man had to wait until the ancestor was alone to attack."

"I want them gone now. None of them can be trusted."

I went into the hut, leaving the boy outside. Crow and his followers were quickly readying to leave. They were rolling up their bedding, which could be used again, and packing in the odd ceramic piece they had traded for while in the village.

"You were right," I said. "My uncle is jumping on the attack to blame all of you."

"We are going, don't worry. If we can leave the settlement in peace, there will be no blood between us. I will find

Boar personally and punish him. For you, the forest is large, but for us, and him, it is small."

"I want you to take my mother with you."

"Your mother?" he asked, stopping what he was doing.

"I have to leave as well. The ancestor is set on returning to my farm. I don't know why, but I want to go back with him, to see to my father. I cannot take my mother, and I cannot leave her here. You saw how my uncle is. He is pulled down by his fear of Wolf Killer. Most of the people here are. They know Wolf Killer could attack, and they do not want to give him any extra reason to do so. If I leave her here, I am afraid of what my uncle would do to her."

"I will take her then. Get her ready now. By the love of White Face and Yellow Face, I will keep her safe for you. Take this." He held out a short flint knife with a stout wooden handle.

"No, Crow, it is too valuable. You should keep it."

"Your uncle should give you a weapon to protect yourself, but he will not. Take the knife. It is only a knife. The Forest People do not hold onto our things. Take it."

I reached out and clutched the knife. Whatever he said, the knife was a valuable item and I was grateful for his kind act. Our hands touched for an instant around the handle. I felt very sorry for him in that moment, having to flee to protect his own band from my people.

He was so young to lead his people, young at least in body, which was lean and strong from a lifetime in the forest, but his eyes showed his true age. He had the years and worries of a true leader. He had a lot more to worry about than me. What was the future to be for his people? All around him, my people, who grew food from the earth, built their big houses, and obsessively watched over their cattle, increased in size, and gnawed at the trees that were so vital to his way of life.

Every year, more trees were cut down for fuel, timber, or to clear the land. What was their life to be if we cut down all the trees? How would they hunt and survive if every animal in the forest was gone? Where would they take rest from the storms if there was no material left to build their hide-covered shelters with?

He smiled, perhaps sensing the moment, until I pulled

my hand free. He turned and issued some commands to his band.

I left them and went to fetch my mother from the hut we had slept in. While I was there, I took some of the flat loaves baked on the hot stones near the fire and shoved them into a woven sack, which I tied around my side. We went back to meet Crow, and all together we walked out of the settlement. I did not bother to say goodbye to my uncle who stood some way off talking loudly to First Calf with his back deliberately toward me. I swore, the next time we encountered each other, I would not show the respect due to a beloved elder.

We managed to get through the settlement without incidence, although some of the armed Lake Men and Women followed us all the way out from the houses and toward the mountain.

At the beginning of the trees above the settlement, I said goodbye to my beloved mother. She was still dejected and numbed by everything that was happening. I was not even sure she was aware I was handing her over to the safe-keeping of Crow. To see her husband killed and her home burnt had all but broken her. I thought on how she had been before all this. She always seemed so happy, ready to help my father with the cattle and crops if she was needed while tending her own jobs around the farm. Her and I had spent whole days working and talking together. She had been a fantastic mother—loving and kind but disciplined when needed.

I hoped that in time she could go some way back to the person she had been. I realized as I held her tight that our roles had now been reversed. Whereas she had been the parent and I the child, now I had to care for her. For the moment, I had to be the strong one in the family. All this was the fault of Wolf Killer, I reminded myself. Wolf Killer destroyed my family, as he had done to others before, and surely he would not stop there. The Lake Settlement was, I knew, despite what my uncle claimed, in real danger. I released her and watched her go with Crow. He brought her away through the trees. I knew he would protect her, not only for me, but because he had promised he would. I turned and nodded to the ancestor.

"Let us return by the path we came," I said. "Over the mountain and home."

Chapter Seven

The man was the second corpse I had seen. My mum being the first. She had been laid out in a coffin in the funeral room, dressed in her best clothes, a wig placed to match her own natural look, with flowers clasped in her hands. She looked peaceful and almost contented. She had lived her life to the fullest, my dad said, having married, had a child, traveled, and worked hard at a good job that she loved. There was no reason to be sad at her parting, he told me. Grandad had made vague references about her having gone to heaven, but did not seem so sure on the matter. I was so young at that time that I did not really comprehend what was happening. I knew she was ill, that she was weak, but as far as I could remember, she had always been that way. I assumed that was just how she was. And then, she was gone. She had died. My dad had tried to prepare me for the event by talking about what happened when people died. He explained how the body stopped working. I had asked where they went when they died, and like Grandad, he had no answer. I did not understand it then and, even now, I still did not. I missed her terribly. Of course, looking back, I also had no idea how hard it was for my dad. I'd never really thought about it until now, but he'd been left with me to raise, a job to hold down, and a house to run on his own. And he had lost his wife. He had never cried, or perhaps I had just never seen him cry.

At least my mother had looked peaceful in her death. Not so this man. He had been flung backward by the force of the arrow. He had not been arranged in death but left with the last fearful grimace on his face. I really felt sorry for the poor girl, but she seemed surprisingly calm. Yes, she cried, but she regained her self-control after a short while. I knelt beside her and tried to comfort her as best as I could, holding her awkwardly, but I really had no idea what to do. She

reached out and stroked the now stretched face of her father. There was no fear of the corpse itself, as if she was
more accustomed to death than I.

And the arrowhead was gone. I had been hoping, expecting, it would still be in the dead man's chest. It would have
been a simple matter of pulling it out and then I was home.
Instead, his chest was open to the air, where his hide top
had been wrenched up around his neck, and a deep hole cut
into the flesh.

"Damn it," I swore softly to myself.

She said some words I could not understand, but it did
not take too much to see that it had been dug out of his
chest probably by the very men who had killed him. Perhaps
arrowheads were too valuable as economic items, considering how long it would take to knap even one, to be left behind. Perhaps they reused all their old arrowheads. Perhaps
they were sick sadists. Whatever the bloody reason, it was
gone and I was still stuck here. She raised a hand and pointed away from the house. I was getting used to her sign language. I guessed she meant it was almost certainly the attackers who indeed had taken the arrowhead with them. I
stood and looked out away from the house in the direction
she had pointed.

This was not the ending I wanted. I did not want to stay
here for the rest of my life. How could I make her understand that I really needed that arrowhead? Would it even be
possible to find it? Did she even know who the attackers
were or where they had come from? I had gathered from the
meeting in the timber house the other night, when the girl
and the two older men had talked and then shouted at each
other, that the attack had been the subject of a robust debate among them. Maybe then they did know the attackers,
maybe it had happened before and this was not some ran-
dom act of violence. At the very least, I assumed they were
arranging a response to the whole event, but this was not
my fight though. I wanted to get home, and to do that, I had
to find that arrowhead.

I turned back to the girl, tapped my own chest, and
waved out over where she had been previously pointing to. I
think she caught on because she stood, glanced over me,
and then and there—how can I describe it—just suddenly

looked really annoyed and determined all at the same time. It was like she had made up her mind. She nodded at me and—the last thing I thought would happen—reached out to pull at my jacket.

Now, I am not a fool. Even without my dad's resolutely straight-faced unashamed yet deeply embarrassing talk some time ago about, as he put it, "men, women, and stuff," I had pretty much gathered from a young age what happened, if not the exact details, in these circumstances. The Internet pretty much showed a person everything they needed to know and some things they did not need to know at all. That said, her pulling at my jacket was not what I expected. I really wished I had a phone connection so I could ring Mick and get his opinion.

I was almost relieved when she then stopped and motioned to her father. She clearly did not have the same thing in mind as I had. Again, she pulled at my jacket and pointed at her father. I could not get what she was trying to say until she bent down by him and pulled at his clothing.

I then got it. *Right*, I thought, *that's no problem. You just want me to strip the clothes from the dead man, take off my own, and put his on. No problem. No problem at all.* I could see what her plan was. Wherever we were going, I had to change my clothes to blend in. She nodded and walked off around the farm, presumably for the sake of modesty while I went over to the body and knelt by him.

"Look," I said. "I am really sorry about this. I am sorry you were killed, and I am sorry I have to take your clothes, but I guess if she thinks it's okay, then you probably wouldn't mind as well."

I reached out and touched his hand. It was cold and almost felt like soft clammy plastic. *Now then*, I said to myself, *this is no time for a weak stomach*. What did Dad always say? Get on with the job, get it done, and think about it later. And he worked in a city hospital where he saw God knows what terrible injuries.

I set about taking off the clothes. The body was stiff and very heavy. I had to pull one arm out from the sleeve and then half-roll and half-lift the man's chest to get the hide top over his head. I stood and pulled at the material to free it from the last arm. It held for a moment and then came off, sending me stumbling back a few feet. After that, I tackled his trousers. That was easier because their clothes were much more basic than we had back home. No zips, buttons, and, I soon discovered, no undergarments. As the girl was still gone, I undressed quickly and put the clothes on. I still had the flint knife I had recovered from the hut in the lake settlement.

Lastly, I pulled off his floppy hide shoes and pulled them up over my bare feet. I then covered his privacy with my own T-shirt as best I could.

To say that his clothes were itchy would be a massive understatement. On top of that, they smelled. I knew they had been worn by a dead man for a few days, but even aside from that, they smelled badly. I got the impression that these people rarely, if ever, washed their clothing.

I gathered up the rest of my clothes and shoes and walked away from the house. I looked around and saw a tuff of tall grass growing by a fence post a short distance away that would make a well-marked hiding place. I dithered a little over the phone. Could I bear to part with it, even though I had only checked it a few times in order to save the battery? My phone was almost an extension of my own body. I felt like I was leaving behind a family member. However, if the girl was intending that we go in disguise to wherever the attackers had come from, it would be pretty stupid if I was found with a phone on me. So, I finally pushed it into the jacket pocket and rolled up the clothes so it was tight in the middle. I parted the grass and shoved the clothes and shoes down against the fence post before closing the grass over again.

After a while, the girl returned and stopped to consider me. Her father's clothes were way too big for me, but she managed somehow, with a few twists here and there, to make them fit reasonably well. She went to the remains of the house and, touching it quickly to make sure it was not too warm, pulled out a piece of burnt plank. She rubbed the timber piece between her hands and smeared my face with the charcoal. Next she drew out a knife and, to my alarm at first, brought it up to my face. She must have seen my look of panic for she smiled to relax me. She then set about cutting my hair, taking off small pieces here and there before smoothing it down. I could not see the result, of course, having no mirror, but figured I now looked more like someone from the settlement by the lake or one of the lads from the forest. I had gone prehistoric. Awesome.

The journey to the farm had taken longer than when we first went over the mountain with Crow. We did not have any guide this time around, so I had to find the paths and ways forward as best I could. I was also worried about Boar, who as far as I knew, was still out there. Crow would find him, of course, but it could take time even for Crow to track an experienced hunter like Boar. In the meantime, he could come looking to finish off what he started.

I kept a steady eye out for him, and anyone else for that matter, during our trek. At night, we split the watches beside the small fire. Finally, however, we came down the mountain and into the farm clearing.

The house was still smoldering, sending a lazy, drifting thin smoke into the air. The roof and walls had collapsed in, leaving behind a warm pile of ash and timber pieces that reached up to my knee. Here and there, along the deep fountain trenches, a piece of planking remained upright to demonstrate how the house had once proudly stood. The animal pen, which had held our precious cattle, was vacant. The Wolf Men had taken the animals with them when they returned to their home by the river. The animals were worth more to them than my father had been. The wheat fields, which had been near ripening for harvesting, had been burnt and left as scorched ground.

My father was still there where he had fallen in front of the house. He lay on his back with his arms and legs spread out as if merely resting after a day's work and watching the clouds float by overhead. The body had not attracted any predators yet, such as the large brooding wolves that lived in the mountains, probably because they were afraid to approach while the house was still burning. A good spell of rain, already threatening on the horizon, would however put out the last of the fire. My father had aged in death since I had last seen him. His skin was taut and yellow. And there was now a large hole in his chest. I looked in and saw that his ribs had been broken and pulled aside. They had removed his heart and the arrowhead.

I sat beside him on the ground and reached out to his rigid hand. I was numbed by seeing him laid out like that. For the first time since the attack, I cried. I wept for my father, my mother, for our home, and for myself. My heart ached at the thought of how he had died, the pain he must have suffered, and I felt an almost identical empty hole inside myself. I cried for what had been, what was, and now what would never be.

The boy came to kneel beside me and pulled me in toward him.

I pressed up against the unfamiliar feel of his smooth clothing and, after a moment, just let myself drape into his arms. I felt that perhaps he would understand better than anyone. After all, he was alone in a place clearly not of his own people and now I too was alone. We both had no one else to rely on.

After a short while, I decided it was time to stop crying. I could have kept up my lament but, here and now, that would not help us. My father would have told me to be strong. He had raised me to be strong.

I pushed away from the boy and wiped away my tears. Besides, I felt another feeling rising up, that of intense anger, toward those who had killed him. There would be a proper time later for grieving. For the moment, I had to separate my feelings of great heartache and the need to carry on living. The boy said something, gestured to the hole in my father's chest and then waved a hand around him. I figured he was referring to the weapon, the arrowhead, which had killed my father, perhaps implying we should look for it around the body.

"The arrowhead is gone," I said, even though I knew he could not understand me. "A weapon that has killed, one that has killed even a wild animal, is very powerful. It has tasted blood and so wants to do so again. It can be remade, re-sharpened, and used over. An arrowhead that has killed a man is far too valuable to be left behind. The Wolf Men took it with them along with his heart so he would not be able to find his ancestor's Stone House. That way, he can't ask our ancestors to punish those responsible for his death."

I pointed away from my father to out over the land where the Wolf Men had returned back to their own settlement. I was sickened by their actions. My father now roamed the Grey Mist looking to find a way to our Stone House on the hill by the lake to be with his own parents and grandparents.

That was why we lit the fires to burn the bodies of the dead and buried the remaining ash and bone fragments in the Stone House. In some ways, it did not really matter what happened to the actual body, it could even be left out in the open for the wolves, once some small part of it was placed in the Stone House. The physical remains served as a torch that shone bright in the Grey Mist to guide the deceased home. But now, as long as the Wolf Men kept my father's heart, he would not be able to find the Stone House. When he came to look for the bright flame in the Grey Mist, there would be two such lights, that of his heart and the remains that normally would have been put in the Stone House. Confused, my father would never have peace.

The boy nodded and said something, grasping that the arrowhead was gone if not fully understanding why, and turned to look where I had gestured. He walked away and stood for a long time, staring in that direction. He then came back, as if having made up his mind. He pointed to me, to himself, and out in the same direction he had been staring.

I was getting more used to interpreting our makeshift signing, so almost at once I realized what he was actually saying. He wanted me to show him where they took the arrowhead. He wanted me to take him to the lair of the Wolf Killer.

I pulled back, a little startled at the idea, until I then saw that he was right. I had to travel to the River Settlement where the Wolf Men lived. The last rites for the dead were normally carried by the whole family, but I was the only one now left to care for my father. I could not rely on my uncle and my mother was in no state to help. It was up to me to retrieve my father's heart so he could find his way home to be with his ancestors.

"If we are to go," I said, standing up, "we have to go suitably dressed. We need to be able to hide in plain view."

I made him understand what I wanted, for him to change clothes with my father, and then left him alone. I wandered off down by the river to find the pots still on the ground where my mother and I had dropped them a few days ago. What should have been a normal day for us, working on the farm, eating, drinking, and then resting as the night came in, had been destroyed by the Wolf Men.

I waited a decent amount of time, walking along the water, and then went back to find the boy dressed in my father's clothes. They were too big for him but would have to do. I made them fit as best I could. I retrieved a suitable chunk of burnt planking from the house pile and studied him.

I marked his face with the charcoal and drew my knife to cut his hair into a style more suitable for a man. "When they think the time is right, the Forest People send their children away to become adults. The child is expected to go into the forest on their own, for how long depends on them, to leave their childhood behind and return as adults. After being out alone in the forest, in order to show that they are full grown, when they return to the rest of the community, they must not speak a word until White Face has dimmed and returned full again. Instead, they must listen, to learn wisdom, to hear the opinions of others, and see that the voice of the community is as important as their own. After their Time of Silence, they become adults and can take their place among the Forest People. After that, they are listened to and can debate with the others as equals."

Once I was finished, he was unrecognizable as the ancestor and looked like one of Crow's band. I held up a closed fist to my mouth as we did to a child when we needed them to be quiet. "You understand, you must remain quiet and no one will know that you do not speak our words. You must remain quiet." I held my fist up to my mouth again.

He smiled and nodded as if getting my meaning. I swung back my closed fist and punched him hard in the shoulder. He let out a shout and I glared at him. He laughed as if saying sorry and pushed his shoulder forward again. I punched him again and this time he was quiet. I nodded my approval. Wherever he was from, they did not breed weak men at least.

I turned and looked around the farm. It was so different

now from the happy memories I had of it with my parents. The place of my childhood had been burnt and smeared with blood. A wind blew down, rising up a few sparks from the house, and I heard an animal call out in the woods beyond.

"Now, we have a long journey ahead of us. The first thing we need to do is get a boat."

Chapter Eight

I had been brought up to believe stealing was wrong. It was always wrong no matter what the circumstances. Well, yes, my dad would perhaps agree with the argument that a man had a right, and even a duty, to steal to feed his starving family. In general, though, ninety-nine percent of the time, stealing was wrong. And to be honest, in this case, I was not stealing to feed anyone. After all, we were taking a boat and not food. Farm Girl, on the other hand, seemed not to have any real trouble with the notion. Maybe, here, rather now, the whole idea of private property was not as quite developed as back home.

After leaving the farm, we had traveled for another two days until reaching a broad full river. I reckoned it was the same river I had seen from the mountain top. We followed the river for another half a day until evening when we came upon a small riverbank settlement. We stopped short of it, near enough, though, to see the boats resting on the gentle sloping sand of the riverbank below the settlement. She signaled for me to be quiet while we went ahead along the bank. We had only gone halfway to the boats, however, when a dog began barking vociferously up at the settlement. She motioned for me to retreat back the way we had come. We then left the riverbank and she took us on a long trek away from the river, through the woods in a great circular path, and back out to the water. We had, I figured, essentially gone around the settlement.

From our new position, we could still see the boats, but this time we were on the other side of them. I thought she would then continue on, that the whole point of the diversion had been to avoid the settlement while sticking to the course of the river, but she now indicated for me to wait on the bank. By this time, the light was getting dim as she, on her own, crept back along the riverbank toward the boats.

She moved slowly. She would steal ahead a foot or so before bending low to merge with the ground. She would then remain motionless for up to ten minutes before rising up to skulk forward once more. I wondered why she was taking so long—why not just run and grab a boat?—when I heard the dog barking again. She squatted and waited until the barking stopped. She was, I then realized, trying to beat the guard dog.

"Pretty smart," I said to myself.

Eventually, as it was getting darker all the while, she reached the first boat, which was resting half in the water and half on the sloping sand tied to a near tree. She hunkered down against its side before popping her head up to take a look inside the boat. Satisfied by what she saw, she moved to the end of the boat and pulled out her knife to cut the rope.

The dog barked up on the bank and she froze against the boat. There were no shouts, however, no alarm being raised, and so she pushed the boat out from the beach. It slid into the water while she pulled herself up and over into the interior. She let it float on for a few feet until raising herself up, just enough so she could see over the rim of the craft. She lowered a paddle over the side. She gently pushed on the paddle, rippling through the water, bringing the boat forward, controlling its direction and moving down to where I waited.

I climbed in, getting my feet wet in the process.

I found a seat in the back of the boat behind her. The "back" probably of course had some sort of technical term like bow, stern, or something, but I had no idea what it was. As silently as possible, we paddled away from the shore while keeping our heads down. It was well past sunset now and looking behind me, I could see the people up on the riverside settlement had lit a large outdoor fire. Men, women, and children were moving back and forth as dark shapes against the growing blaze. I just hoped they stayed up on the bank away from the river until we were safely away. Even though I knew next to nothing about rivercraft or sailing, I could tell that the boat, more of a canoe really, was a fine vessel and one they would not wish to part with. It was around fifteen feet in length and appeared to be a single piece of timber. That meant it had been chipped out from one particular tree trunk. It must have taken ages to make. I was starting to appreciate, the longer I was here, that practically everything these people owned was a one-off and in some ways unique item that had taken time and resources to produce. They did not have the option of simply going down to the shops or online to buy new products when the old one broke. For starters, money had not been invented yet. I supposed all the same that they had other boats tied up on the shore. At least they would not starve if they could not go fishing in the morning. That is what I told myself, still nevertheless, I was stealing from them and I felt bad about it.

We glided through the water. The sound of the settlement died away, and the girl sat up fully with both arms over one side, sweeping the paddle into the water. I made to follow suit with the paddle lying in front of me on the bottom of the boat, but she turned and shook her head, meaning for me to wait. So, instead, I dipped a hand in the water and brought a palmful up to taste it. I wondered if at home the same river was still there. I remembered from Geography class that rivers often changed their course over time. If it was still there, I wondered how polluted it was by that stage.

We went on through the night. After a while, she turned and nodded at me. It was my go. At first the paddle was a little unwieldy, but after a short time, I got the hang of it. She meanwhile rolled herself up and, in a while, I heard her breathing become heavier, indicating she had fallen asleep. I kept the canoe as best I could to the middle of the river and, in truth, once I hit a stride, it was not so hard. More akin to steady regular exercise than anything too strenuous.

The riverbanks on either side of me came alive with the nocturnal creatures inhabiting the forest that grew thick out over the water. It was equally quiet and noisy at the same time. At one point, I leaned back in the canoe and stared upward. There were no artificial lights out here, so I could see the whole of the massive Milky Way stretched above us, as if mirroring our course, like a sparkling river of the night sky. I had never seen it so clear and bright before. I found it quite pleasant to be there, after all the activity of the last few days, to be alone, just with her, on the water.

After what seemed a few hours or so, she stirred and pulled herself up. She glanced over her shoulder to make sure I was still there and took up her own paddle. She said something and dropped her head. Sleep. It sounded like a good idea, but how could I sleep in these circumstances? I was too used to having a bed. Nevertheless, I slipped forward onto the bottom of the boat and rested my head on my arm on the seat. I must have been more tired than I thought for, as I dozed off, I heard her paddle enter the water and begin the slow rhythmic slosh.

The boy woke, looked around, and then pulled himself back up onto his seat. I had let him sleep well into the morning. I had just been wondering if we should have some of the last food in the sack, so I broke off my paddling.

The canoe slowed down slightly. We had done well, never breaking our journey through the night, and had traveled far more than we could have done over land. That would have taken days and meant heading through deep forests. All the while, we would have had to avoid the wolves, bears, and people between us and our destination. Taking the boat would have made my father angry and he would have said as such to me. However, it was faster and safer to travel by water.

I looked in the sack and brought out the remaining bread. I turned around to the boy to pass back a loaf when an arrow landed with a soft thud in the bottom of the canoe between us. He stared at the arrow as if wondering where it possibly could have come from, thinking perhaps that he was still asleep and was dreaming.

I looked over his shoulder and saw the other canoe some way down the stretch of the river. There was a man standing up in the fore end of the craft, holding the bow, and squinting to see if his shot had hit home. His aim was off by an arrow's length or so, because I had rested for a moment. The archer had obviously gauged his shot on our and their respective paces. If I had not have stopped paddling, he would not have missed.

"They found us," I said. "And they want their canoe back."

I dropped the bread and began to paddle furiously. After a moment, I felt the canoe surge forward as the ancestor joined me. I glanced over my shoulder and saw that the archer had sat down again and joined his companion at paddling. They had managed to sneak up on us and had probably decided to take a chance before they came within earshot. If the arrow hit, all the better, and if it missed, well, we would have heard their paddles sooner or later. I leaned forward and put my back into it. After a few moments, our strokes matched up, pushing the canoe on faster.

On one side I dipped in, brought the paddle back over to the other side, and heaved again. If the two men behind had traveled the same length of the river as us, and considering the time they would have lost until someone from their settlement noticed the missing craft, it probably implied both of them had been going hard all night. That meant, with any luck, they were not as rested as us. On the other hand, they had probably spent their entire lives on the river and were far more used to the water than either me or the ancestor.

It had been a risk taking the canoe. I had hoped to put a greater distance between us and the rightful owners before they discovered our actions. I kept my eyes on the river ahead, pulling myself away from the distraction of looking back continuously. All that did was slow us down and showed the face of our fear to the chasing men. If they caught up with us, the archer would almost certainly order a halt and fire off another arrow. However, if we kept moving, keeping the same approximate distance between us, they would not be able to break for a second shot as even a few moments of their wasted time could give us the advantage. *Keep going*, I said to myself. *Do not stop.*

Yellow Face rose higher in the sky. The shade retracted from the trees and the light fell onto the river. It got hotter very quickly. My arms began to twinge, but I refused to give in. I refused to listen to the pain demanding that I stop and rest. I remembered my poor father, alone and unable to find his way to his ancestor's Stone House. Was he afraid? Did he not want to meet again with his own mother and father? I thought of him and I thought of the man who ordered his death. The raw anger rose in me, feeding the strength in my arms, forcing me not to slack but to dip the paddle into the water, pull it back, and repeat.

On and on we went as the water began to dazzle me. The glittering radiance of Yellow Face falling onto each wave and ripple was almost blinding. I lowered my face and pulled on the paddle again. Would we sail on the river forever, past the settlement of the Wolf People, past the edge of the land, and out into the other Wide Water some said was at the end of the land? Would we sail on until we reached the brink of the water itself and fall down amid a mighty waterfall into whatever was beyond?

I heard the ancestor breathing behind me. I wondered if he was getting tired, but I knew that he would not give in. He would go on as long as I did. If only, I thought, this boy really was one of my ancestors. He could have waved a hand and stopped them in their tracks. As Yellow Face moved toward his plinth above us, the woods on the riverbanks cleared and we broke through to low grass lands.

I glanced around to see that they were gaining on us. They only thing they probably wanted more than their canoe back was to catch the thieves who stole it. I returned to my task and then saw something which gave me heart. A single cow stood on the riverbank, coming down to fill his gut with the river water, staring as we went by. A cow meant there was a herd somewhere, a herd meant there was a farm, a farm meant a settlement, and a settlement meant people. In this case, the Wolf People.

As if in acknowledgement, I heard a sharp splash behind us. I looked and saw that the archer was standing again in his boat. He too had seen the cow and knew what it meant. We had reached the beginning of the land of the Wolf People and he dare not go any farther. He loosened another arrow, but it fell well short of the mark. He lowered the bow and looked on as we slipped ahead. I respected him for that. He had lost us and the canoe, but even in his anger he did not fire off a useless volley of valuable arrows.

We pushed on, saved by our enemy, deeper into the den of the grey beast, toward their main settlement.

Chapter Nine

What had I been expecting? I did not know. I can say with certainty, though, I had not been expecting what we found. I had been assuming our destination would be like the settlement by the lake. Equal in size to the compact collection of houses and small farms there. I figured that the people who attacked the girl's home were from another similar type of settlement. That they had burnt the isolated house to show their warrior's prowess or something like that. What we actually found, what we came on, was very different. The settlement was enormous compared to the one by the lake. It started soon after the lads in the other boat had given up and let off a few arrows in annoyance at us. I was glad they gave up when they did because I was exhausted. I had fallen into a trance with the paddle—in, out, in, out—but I surprised myself. My dad would have been proud of me for not quitting. And to be honest, I figured if she could keep going, then so could I.

The first house we came upon was perched on the high riverbank, and I wondered if it had been placed in that particular location so as to keep an eye on the river. A small boy, only wearing a cloth wrapped around his waist, was standing on the bank watching us approach. He shouted and a man appeared at his side. They stared as we went past but did not call out or make any move toward us. After the first house, the river broadened and more and more signs of habitation appeared along its banks. Houses were planted either on their own or in groups. Children played in and around the river. The air was filled with the smell of burning fires while people worked on the riverbank or the fields behind, mingling with the cattle and sheep who browsed on the thick grass growing there. A few fishing craft with one or two people also cruised by. The occupants glanced over and then ignored us.

Ahead, the river went into a slow, lazy curve and we followed the water as it swept around. I saw that the girl, who until then had been paddling as if undisturbed by the people on either side of her, stopped in her efforts. Other than the occasional dip to correct the course of the canoe, she let the river take us.

As we came out from the curve, I nearly dropped the paddle into the water in amazement at what lay before us. On the right bank, a huge, towering, straight-sided mound, more of a hill really, sat on the crest of a rise and glittered in the afternoon light. It was some way up from the river but still clearly visible as the land in the bend of the river moved away from us in a gentle upward slope.

As we got nearer and changed our relative positioning on the water, the shimmering effect died away. I could then see that it was caused by the sunlight reflecting on white stones placed in a dispersed pattern into the side of the mound.

Looking closer, I saw that one side of the artificial mound was not as steep as the rest and the bare earth and rocks underneath were still visible. A group of men were moving among a tangled mess of loose branch scaffolding and platforms around this section. Whether they were still building the mound or repairing it, I could not tell. Of course, I knew as well that it was not actually a mound as such but rather a tomb. Larger than the one at the lake settlement, but still basically a similar type of structure. I knew this because on seeing the mound, I recognized exactly where we were.

This time, I could identify our location not because my grandad was a renowned archaeologist or because I had seen it in one of his books. Rather, in my time, this site represented one of the country's top tourist destinations. People came from all over the world to be bussed out to the adjacent interactive interpretative center. They came to see the great tomb mound, have their photo taken in front of it, and finish off the day with some lunch in the nearby restaurant.

There was a number of smaller grass mounds placed haphazardly around the large central structure. All of the mounds were in turn surrounded by a great circle of tall wide standing stones. After the outer stone circle, the entire bend of the river was occupied by an assorted collection of houses and huts, fields, fences, animal pens, other smaller mounds, wide circles of flat-toped banks, single isolated standing stones, and paths running throughout the entire settlement.

The girl muttered something and I could only agree. Someone shouted and we looked to the near riverside beach we were approaching. A man was waiting there, among the canoes and fish drying racks. He held up a hand, gesturing us toward him. He looked like he thought he was important.

I climbed out of the boat and held the man's hand to my forehead. He allowed the gesture of respect but quickly pulled the hand away from me when I was finished. As if he did not want to touch me for too long. He went down to the water's edge and inspected the canoe. He saw the arrow still standing upright in the bottom of the canoe.

"Where did you get it?" he asked.

"We took it," I said.

"From one of the settlements down the river?"

"Yes."

"Those settlements owe us allegiance. They belong to us."

"Then I am only retuning your boat."

"What do you want here?"

"We have heard tales of the great Wolf People. We have come to ask to join with you."

"You're from the forest?"

"Yes."

"And where are your own people? Why did you leave them?"

"My father said I couldn't be with my man, the two of us should not be together. It was forbidden, he said, so we left. Besides, we are tired of living like animals. The Forest People are dying and cannot provide for us anymore. I heard of how great the Wolf People are, and we want to join with you. My man is undertaking his Time of Silence and soon he will be a true man, but he is ambitious. He does not want us to live in a cramped hovel in the forest anymore."

"In other words, you ran away. You're alone."

"Yes."

"The Wolf People can welcome you," he said, looking more closely over us. "You both seem young and strong. You managed to steal a boat, showing you're clever at least. We can take you in, if you are useful that is. We have no space for idle persons here."

"My man can fight. I can track."

"We have plenty of trackers, but we always need more fighters. A wolf pack always needs more wolves. We will see. Go up the bank to the fire there and say the man on the beach sent you. They will give you food. Then come down here to sleep by the boat for the night."

"Yes, thank you."

"In the morning, we will see if you are of any worth to us. I would spend the night beseeching White Face to make sure you are useful." The man turned and walked back up to the settlement.

I signaled for the boy to get out. We pulled the canoe up a little up onto the beach beside the others already there. There was a large hazel tree growing out over the beach with ropes hanging off its lower branches, so I tied one of them to the canoe. We had arrived at the land of the Wolf Killer. I was thrilled that our disguise had worked so well, but still felt jumpy at being here. We had come this far, though, and could not stop now.

Together, we left the beach and went up to the settlement beyond. We found the central fire easily enough. A large crowd of the Wolf People was gathered around it, sitting on the ground or log stools, eating and drinking as the night came in. Gangs of children were running and messing with each other as children did everywhere. A low table, cut from a single split tree truck, was positioned near the fire. It held joints of cooked meat laid out on a platter of leaves and ceramic bowls containing water and cider.

I did not know what I had been expecting, but this was not it. I had never imagined that the Wolf People would be like everyone else. I assumed them to be more malevolent. Instead, as we walked over to the food, I saw a man sitting with a child on his lap. He laughed as he and his friends shared a joke. As we got nearer, I looked closer at the man and saw a long, deep scar had been scratched into his arm. I recognized the cutting of a flint knife when I saw it. The man had been badly injured in a fight but had healed. Perhaps the man was not a farmer but a fighter, a warrior, and I wondered if he had been one of the men who had attacked and burnt my farm. He looked up, saw my gaze, which I dropped, and went back to his own circle.

A large stout man was sitting by the table. I explained we had been sent up from the beach. He flicked a head toward the food as if he was used to strays feeding off them. I was starving by now and even the smell of the food was distracting. I quickly cut off a large chunk of meat, waiting at any moment for the man to tell me I was taking too much. I slipped it onto a leaf and we hurried away down to the beach. We ate, side by side, sitting on the sand, staring out over the water where the swallows were circling in wide graceful circles to catch the evening insects.

It was actually quite peaceful there with only the sound of water. I found myself thinking about my mother and hoping she was all right and not missing me. I stood and went down to the river where I knelt to wash the grease of the meat off my hands and take a drink of the cool water. When I returned to the canoe, I saw that the boy had already lain out on the sand and was fast asleep. We were both exhausted after the long day that we had. I wondered what tomorrow would bring. I lay down on the beach, near him, and was soon asleep myself.

Chapter Ten

I felt the kick on my back and could barely stop myself from letting out a shout. I had had not really slept that well. It was cold at night by the river and we had no blankets to cover us. I had only dozed here and there, with dreams of rushing water and tall looming mounds, and so was still awake when they came for me. I rolled myself around in the sand and squinted up at the three smiling lads standing in a circle around us. My first thought was to wonder if the girl was all right.

The nearest lad, who had probably been the one that kicked me, barked an order. The other two grabbed me and pulled me up from the sand. I struggled with them, and as much to my astonishment as his probably, managed to break free from one of them and push him back with my free hand. He snarled, jumped at me, and seized my arm tighter this time. They dragged me down to the river and heaved me in. I landed in the freezing water, sending a shock through my body.

I tried to stand but was roughly forced down again by the two lads who had followed me into the water. I thrashed out against their hold, hitting something, for one of the lads let go. This allowed me to squirm my way free from the other's grip and to kick out with both feet to swim a few feet out from the bank. Thinking that I had gone far enough to get clear of them, I twisted around in the water to stand. I felt the slimy mud underfoot but succeeded in getting a foot holding.

The lads were advancing on me again through the water until a command from the one on the bank, their leader obviously, stopped them and they turned back. The leader then gestured for me to come over. I remained where I was for a few moments, wet through, until waddling to the bank. I could hardly stay in the river all day after all. He nodded at me and clapped a hand tight onto my shoulder. He then held up a finger and indicated I was to follow him. As we went past the girl, who had come down to the water to witness the whole event, I nodded and smiled at her. I wanted to reassure her I was fine after my ordeal.

The leader brought me up to the large fire, now burning low, where we had gotten the food last night. At this time of the morning, the hearth area was deserted save for a few other lads around my age who looked up at my arrival as if taking in my worth. I knew then what had happened, why the two goons had thrown me in the river and where I was. That had been a test, to see if I would fight back, and this was a schoolyard. Admittedly, at a different type of school than the one I was used to, no problem using corporal punishment it seemed, but still a school nevertheless.

There was food, flat sour bread, and some green stew. I ate while taking in my fellow pupils. I had no idea what I was signing myself up for, but if Farm Girl thought we needed to be here, and after we had gone through such trouble to get here, it was obvious I needed to make a good impression.

Not being able to speak, even if I had wanted to, was an advantage over the coming days. The few times anyone in the group tried to say something to the two goons or question an order from the leader, they just received a punch as an answer. We soon learned to stay quiet. After our first breakfast, our training, or selection process—I suppose that was the best way to describe it—began.

The leader gave a quiet order after the meal was finished and set off at a run. We followed because there seemed little else to do. We ran along the beach, climbed up onto the riverbank where the grass began, and left the settlement behind. We passed through the outer fields and animal holds surrounding the settlement into the woodland beyond.

I guess that the almost constant physical activity since I had arrived had burned off some of the puppy fat. Perhaps I knew I had to prove myself in order to be allowed to remain in their settlement so as to have any hope of retrieving the arrowhead. Possibly, I was just stubborn and had no intention of letting the other lads get the better of me. Whatever the reason, then and there as I jogged along, I decided that whatever they wanted, no matter how much they pushed, I would never give in or quit.

When I was younger, I used to love playing football. I was not very good at it, but I was not too bad either. My dad said to me one day after watching me play that he was proud of me. I never really got what he meant. We had lost the game and, even though I had given my best, I knew I had played pretty bad that day. I think I kind of now understood what he was getting at. It was not necessarily how good or bad a person was at something; what was really important was that they never gave up. The effort to succeed could be the key to succeeding. *A little corny*, I thought, *but true*.

We went farther and farther into the woods, which were full of early morning bird song. The sun threw a cast of flickering shadows through the tree tops. The leading lad out front seemed to have endless stamina. Here and there we found a path and followed that until, perhaps deciding the pace was getting too easy, he veered off and went into the tree cover again.

I kept going, but one of my fellow trainees beside me grew increasingly short-breathed and then fell away. While one of the two goons stopped to lambast him, the rest of us continued on among the bushes and thorns. They tore at our clothing and hands as we jumped over trees that had fallen and scrambled up inclines.

I felt I was near to bursting. I could not draw another breath or cover another step when the leader stopped in the middle of a clearing in the woods. I came to a halt and took a deep breath but did not throw myself on the ground as some of the others did. I looked around at the other lads in the clearing and thought, *I am ready for this*.

The first number of days was taken up with more exercises such as cross county running and even swimming in the river. I was not the greatest swimmer, but some of the lads in the group were hopeless. One of them even had no idea how to swim, having obviously never learned. He just stood in the cold water, watching us swim to the far bank. Wherever he was from, clearly not from the settlement by the river, there had been nowhere around that he could learn to swim. Maybe he was from high up in the mountains or from the forest. Reaching the far bank, we pulled ourselves out from the water and, even with our sodden garments, we set off on another run. *At least*, I thought, *my clothes are finally getting a good wash.*

At night, after each exhausting day, we were taken to a camp in an overgrown fallow field in the middle of the busy settlement. Camp may have been an over generous description. There was no fire nor were we given any bedding or blankets. We were expected to sleep on the open grass. It was made clear that we should not leave the field, although they did not bother to guard us. We could see the other people around us as they finished off the last of their daily tasks. The men went by looking us over and laughing. Women walked by ignoring us while the children played endlessly.

There was nothing to do from when they dropped us off in the field in the evening until they came to pick us up again in the morning. The boredom was as hard to bear as the cold. Tantalizingly nearby, we could see the settlement fires being brought back to full life each evening. When it got dark, it was worse because we could see the people gathering around the open fires to eat, drink, laugh, sing, and relax. Simple food, consisting of more of the hard, flat, sour bread loaves and some thin soup in wooden bowls, was brought to us after dark. A single animal water skin was dropped on the ground the first night. We were expected to share out the water as we saw fit and fill it ourselves from the river. As no one else took on the job, I did it myself every day, often passing by the leader and his goons as they ate their better fare.

This was, I figured, part of the test, of course. They put us in the middle of the settlement so we would see the comforts and warmth of fire and family life around us. They wanted us to suffer. I guessed in some ways it was easier for me. It was a strange culture to me, so being in the field or by one of the fires was equally unique for me. I was already away from my home either way. I could see, though, that some of the other boys were greatly affected by it. Perhaps, this was the first time they had been cut off from their families.

I was not surprised one morning when I noticed that one of them was gone. He had snuck off home in the middle of the night. The leader, when he returned, if he even noticed, seemed unbothered by it. *He wants us to break*, I reckoned. *He wants us to feel homesick, hungry, and tired. He does not care if we leave. He only wants those that stay, those that are strong.*

Chapter Eleven

The first morning in the River Settlement, I watched as the warrior set dragged the ancestor out from the side of the canoe and threw him into the water. I stood and could only look on as he thrashed against the two men. It was his fight and there was nothing I could do to help him. As he fought his way up to stand on his two feet and stood glaring at his assailants, I was relieved. I knew at that point that he was capable of looking after himself. I actually felt a little proud of him. As they led him away, he turned to smile at me as he went by. He was gone and we were both on our own.

After the abrupt awakening, I washed myself in the river and ate the remainder of the food from the previous night. I doubted anyone would come for me. The entire warrior set had been male, I had noticed. I squatted on the sand by the river and wondered what my next move should be. Why was I even here? What did I hope to achieve? In the cold morning, I remembered the anger I had felt as we were paddling hard to escape the archer on the river. I was surprised by the depth of my rage. Had I just come to find my father's heart, to guide him home through the Grey Mist, or was that really a pretext for my true reason for coming here? What did I want? Justice for my father? What did that entail, however, finding Wolf Killer and seeking reattribution? Was I even capable of that? I still did not really know why I had come.

I spent the rest of the overcast morning around the settlement. I had been startled, I had to admit, to find that the Wolf People were no different from my own. They went about their everyday chores the same as the people at the Lake Settlement. And yet, there was something different about the place. For starters, the settlement was huge by the standard of the Lake Settlement. At first, that seemed a little daunting. How could people live like this, I wondered, all cramped up against each other in their houses sitting amid mounds, work huts, and animal pens? In the Lake Settlement, no matter where a person was standing outside, they could almost always see the lake or the countryside around the settlement. On my farm, we had been totally surrounded by the wild forest. Here I was cut off, for the first time in my life, from a view of the natural world.

As I walked around, getting a grasp of the layout of the settlement, I kept away from the people going about their tasks. They, in turn, seemed happy to keep away from me. That was another odd thing. A stranger approaching the Lake Settlement would have been surrounded in moments by people wanting to know their names, where they came from, and their business being there. If they were passing though or trading, they would have been made welcome, but if not, they would have been forced out. Here, though, no one approached me asking questions about my presence. They seemed, if not welcoming of strangers, almost indifferent.

I wandered into the center of the settlement where the paths became tighter and the structures more compacted on each other. I noticed, the farther in I went, there were more men carrying weapons while there were less women and children around.

I then came across the timber palisade. A towering wall of posts, made from stout felled trees, dug deep into the earth. It spread out from either side of me and ran away in a great circle. It sat atop a small rise in the center of the settlement and was entered by a gateway formed by two larger timber pillars. The gateway was guarded by two men holding axes.

Beyond the gate, I could see a range of buildings of differing sizes sitting on varying ground levels. They were connected by short sections of wooden steps laid into the earth. Without a doubt, I had discovered the home of the Wolf Killer. The few people who came and went while I was there were all stopped and looked over by the men at the gate. I knew I could not just brazen my way in. Their indifference to strangers did not extend to the area beyond the palisade.

I drifted away from the gate, not wishing to draw too much attention to myself, and decided instead to check out the Stone House, which was situated back toward the river. As I got nearer to the mound, it seemed to grow in height and width until its presence blocked out everything around it. I had never seen anything like it in my life. The sheer size dwarfed the Stone House of the Lake Settlement. It was truly astounding. I would not have believed it possible for mere people to build such a monumental edifice if I had not seen it with my own eyes.

The shouts and calls of the workmen clambering around the unfinished section wafted out over the grass area surrounding the mound. I wondered how long had they been working on it. Surely, its construction must have begun years ago even before Wolf Killer was born. And what was its purpose? A Stone House that large was extravagant. It was grandiose beyond necessity. It spoke not of an honest desire to provide a comfortable abode for the dead of the community, but rather of the ambition of the living to demonstrate their own power. Who were these Wolf People to display such arrogance in all that they did?

Keeping a distance out from the mound, I walked around its periphery until finally coming to the entrance into the interior. There was an avenue of stones leading to and guarding the square opening, which seemed almost comically small in comparison to the rest of the huge mound. I wondered if that was deliberate? After all, a cramped entrance meant it was easier to control who was allowed to enter the passageway beyond. Near the entranceway, I saw a crowd gathered around one of the smaller adjacent mounds. They were listening to a central figure on the top. I went closer and recognized the figure as a shaman. She was dressed differently from the shaman at the Lake Settlement, but carried herself in the same manner with exaggerated intense actions. Her clenched hands were raised upward to the sky. Out of curiosity, I moved through the crowd to listen to what she was saying.

"Yellow Face, shine down on us," she called out. "See our efforts and give us your blessings, we ask you, make your people strong and unbending, make them fierce, and make our flint hard. Let the command of the Wolf People go out through the whole land and bring all the settlements together as one. Guide the great Wolf Killer in this noble and just cause, make the Wolf People the strongest of all. Let the whole land obey us. Let..."

The crowd around me, consisting of men, women, and even small children, were murmuring their approval at each of her supplications. To be honest, I was a little taken aback by what she was saying. Why was she calling on Yellow Face to help them conquer other peoples?

As far as I knew, Yellow Face and White Face chased each other through the firmament, day and night, trying to be close to one another, which they only achieved on those rare occasions that White Face finally caught up with Yellow Face. Then the land went dark in the middle of the day as they came together. People often called on them for assistance with animals, crops, or other day-to-day concerns, but I had never heard anyone ask them to assist in destroying an enemy or to make other people suffer. Why would they do that?

I wondered what other strange beliefs the Wolf People held. What of their ancestors? My people thought that, in times of great crisis, a person's ancestors could possibly reach out from the Grey Mist which bounded all the Stone Houses. If inclined to, the ancestors could provide help or seek justice for a great wrong, but not bring sorrow to others. Beyond the ancestors, there was the more obscure and enigmatic Originator. When the world was covered by water, the Originator had dreamt of the land along with the multitude of animals, fish, birds, and people. Would the Wolf People likewise appeal to the Originator to help them in their deeds of conquest? This was something I had never heard of.

The crowd grew more excited as the shaman went on. They pressed forward to be closer to the mound. I was dragged in with them and was jostled as they packed in around me. Their murmurings became louder and a few began to break into shouts. The throng was getting more and more agitated as the shaman lead them on. I was starting to feel hemmed in by the scrum pressing against me.

A sudden sensation that I would be crushed by the crowd took hold of me. I felt that I needed to get away from them as quickly as possible. My breathing became shallow and my hands gritted tight. I turned to find a solid wall of bodies, but I had to get out. I brought up both hands together and used them as a wedge to force an opening between the bodies. After a moment, the wall parted slightly and I squeezed myself into the gap. I kept on going, driving a way through the horde. My head was starting to hurt and my vision blurred around the edges. I wondered if I was going to faint, fearing that the crowd in their animated mood would then trample me underfoot. Finally, I made it to the edge of the crowd and was able with one last thrust to burst out into the open space beyond.

I moved away from the mound area altogether and came to a stop some way off to get my bearings. I breathed in and out slowly. After a while, my vision returned to normal. My hands were still a little shaky, so I closed my eyes and thought of my mother in order to relax.

"Are you all right, girl?" a voice asked.

I looked around for the person speaking and saw an old woman, standing behind a nearby timber fence, looking at me with concern.

"Yes," I said. "I'm fine."

"You're shaking."

"I'm fine now."

"You were up listening to those idiot shamans?"

"Yes."

"You should stay away from them. They talk a lot of non-sense these days. Come here then, if you're all right. I need some help."

I walked to the fence and looked over to see the woman was standing ankle deep in mud while a number of piglets ran around her. Her hands and clothes were covered in the mud. I guessed that whatever she was trying to achieve with the pigs, she was failing.

"Are you all right?" I asked her.

"No, I am not," she said, and laughed. "I can't catch the little runt. Can you help me?"

I climbed over the fence of the sty and stepped down into the mud. I knew that it would take an age for me to get the dirt off my clothes.

"Thank you, thank you," she said. "You're filthy now, like me."

"Which one do you want?"

"That one there, the little one, the runt. He's not growing and he's eating too much. He's stopping the others from getting big and fat. He's small but fast. He keeps running away when I go near him."

"You go behind him and herd him to me."

The woman followed my instructions, separating the smallest piglet from the rest by kicking the air. Together, we managed to force him into one of the corners of the sty. I let him rest there for a moment. When he started to ignore us and went back to putting his snout in the mud, I went forward slowly. I kept my arms tight by my sides and, only when I was within arm's reach did I grab him with both hands and squeeze him tight against my chest. He struggled at first, wriggling to be free, but after a few moments when it was clear I would not be letting go, he settled down, resigned to his captivity.

"Where do you want him?"

"Here, in the basket."

I brought him over and deposited him into the woven basket. The woman brought the lid down hard. She passed a stick through an outer grass loop on the basket rim, into a loop on the lid, and out the matching loop on the far side. The piglet was secured.

"Thank you," she said again. "I don't recognize you. You're not from here?"

"No."

"You're one of the Forest People, are you?"

"Yes."

"Come down from the hills to join us. I never can understand why you folk come here. What I would give to live up there with you, running free like I did when I was a girl, but I guess you're young. You want more than just to be free. Come on then, help me with the basket and we can have something to eat."

"Where are you taking it?"

"It's for the feast. The chief is giving a big feast in a few days for some important visitors. They want the animals brought in now."

"I don't understand you. Who's giving the feast?"

"The chief."

"What is a...chief?"

"You really are from the forest. The chief, the great and wonderful Wolf Killer, such a ridiculous name. Not even his real name, you know, but don't tell anyone I said that. He's the leader here. These are his pigs. He owns them along with all the other animals here, along with me as well."

"Sorry," I said in amazement. "He owns you?"

"Yes."

"How can he own you? You can't own a person."

"Maybe not in the forest, but here you can. I'm a slave. And before you ask, it means I'm not free. Yes, he owns me. I work for him. I tend these pigs."

"I still don't understand."

"I barely do myself, dear girl. What's your name?"

"Spring Bloom," I lied.

"My name is New Water. I'll bring you home first so you can get cleaned up. Then we can bring the little runt up to the chief's hall."

Chapter Twelve

The longer I spent around the group of lads, the more differences I was able to spot between them. There were some obvious cultural ones like the clothing and haircuts, but also subtler personal differences. I even gave a few of them nicknames based on their oddities.

One of the lads would always sit on the ground when eating, so I called him Grounder. Another, I called Bread Boy, because he would never eat the type of bread we were served. There was one lad who appeared permanently to be on the verge of laughing. He had an upturned smile most of the time. I called him Laughter Dude. Another seemed forever to be in a bad mood who was hence nicknamed Grumpy Git.

The impression I got after a few days was that while most of them were probably from the settlement on the river, others had come from distant parts to join up with the group. That would make sense. I guessed that in every age, young people were always driven to seek out adventure. I doubted any of them had come farther than me, though. No matter where they were from, however, the leader and his two goons treated us all equally. No favors were shown to anyone. As the days went on, a few more of them found the endless regular activities hard going and our number continued to dwindle.

The regime of exercises we went through was designed to push us to our physical limits, but it was more than just that. They wanted to mentally squeeze us. To see if we could take the pain and keep going. To test our minds as well as our bodies. There were other less obvious trials to determine how we reacted in given situations.

One afternoon, we were taken to what seemed an empty field. We stood on one side of the dry stone wall. The leader pointed across to the other side of the field. We all climbed over the wall, including the leader and his men, and set off at a slow trot across the grass. I could not see the difficulty of the exercise. It seemed easy, until I heard a pounding behind us. I turned to see a full-grown brown bull, which had been resting unnoticed in one corner of the field, charging toward us in a fury that we had dared enter his domain. We scattered in panic. I shot off for the far wall. I cleared the distance in a few seconds and scrambled over. The others all made it safely over, and after a moment, one of them laughed. Soon, we had all joined in. The leader smiled at our behavior. He seemed pleased at our laughter. We were not laughing at the bull, of course, who still circled the field in front of us, but at ourselves. Fear, it seemed, was relative. We had not known the bull was there and so had not been afraid to go into the field.

There were also maneuvers that I thought at first were intended as team building actions to bond us a group. One morning, we were awoken unusually earlier than normal from our field and got up on our feet. The leader held up a blanket, which he wrapped around his hand and then set off at a jog into the light-edged darkness. The two goons made us wait for around twenty minutes before we moved out after him. It was obviously a game of chase. The leader had the tag. I hung back in the middle of the running pack. After all, I had absolutely no tracking skills of any kind and that would have been obvious if I had taken the lead.

One of the other lads had no such problem and, probably delighted to finally stand out from the rest of us, took point while we followed. We left the settlement as normal, but struck off in a new direction. I knew the leader could easily have outpaced any of us if he had so wished. He could also probably have passed over the terrain without leaving a single trace. He clearly wanted us to be able to track him. We left the flat lands of the river plain and headed up a low hill.

As we peaked the top of the hill, we ran straight into the glare of the rising sun. The new day's light streaked out over a spattered expanse of orange-lit slush pools dotted with small patches of tufted dry scrubland and twisting trees. It was actually quite beautiful to see the marshland on the other side of the hill so early in the morning. Well, I thought it was, but the appearance of the marsh had a dramatic and sudden unexpected effect on the rest of the group. Without even waiting for the tracker to lead, some of the lads in the group broke formation and veered away from the top of the hill. They ran back down the ascent we had just climbed. It was as if the marsh held a tangible, terrifying fear for them. I guess that would make some sense. Without any modern maps, G.P.S. units, phones, and other safety gear, a marsh represented a huge danger where a person could easily get lost and sucked down. Leaving no trace behind. Still, though, it was odd that they were so alarmed by its mere presence that they had to immediately escape from its vicinity. There was another lesson here, I figured. There was a reason why the leader had taken us so close to something he knew would scare us, or them at least. Maybe he was telling us that no matter how brave and strong we were, there was always something worse out there.

After the first few days, when the weaker members of the band were weeded out, we also took part in more specific military type training with weapons. This time, I failed publicly. It was clear that the others had been around the weapons we were using since birth. I, on the other hand, had no experience whatsoever with spears, stone axes, bows-and-arrows, clubs, or flint knives, other than the usual not very practical video and app games at home. I knew I had to fit in nevertheless and tried my best.

The handheld weapons were not so bad, to be honest. They were clearly blunt for the purpose of the exercises and were designed only to bruise rather than actually cut the skin. Split into groups of two out in the woods, we were given various weapons and commanded to go at it. Among the bustle of the group, I think I managed to hide my inexperience as best I could.

My first bout was with axes against the Laughter Dude. He smiled and came at me head on. He clearly reckoned he could shock me into submission. Maybe that was how he treated his little brother back home, but he was wrong if he thought it would work on me. I stood my ground. His shoulder whacked into me and we both went tumbling down into the dry dirt. He jumped up and, with that smile still on his face, reached out a hand to help me up. After that, after getting the first blow over and done with, it was actually not so bad. Every lad seemed to have a different technique. While Laughter Dude tried to rush his opponent, Grumpy Git liked to stay out of arm's reach and then go for a killing blow. Bread Boy always just looked scared and would hit out blindly while Grounder seemed to work himself up into a rage and then go berserk. In some ways, being so inexpert, it was almost easier for me. I could learn and adapt to their fighting skills while not being stuck in my own rigid methods.

Even with blunt weapons, I realized early on that I had to be as concerned with getting hurt as hurting my opponent. I found, with the hand-held weapons at least, that the fights often quickly descended into schoolyard wrestling matches. I gave as good as I got. I was beaten a few times, thrown to the ground, but with increasing frequency, I managed to hold my opponent to a rough draw or even best him. To my great surprise, I even started to look forward to the bouts. We would spend the day in the usual exercises, but evening was when the real fun started. After a day or two, I began to ignore the bruises and cuts. I found I enjoyed testing myself, and I wanted to see if I could win.

Where I failed miserably, and where it was definitely noticed by everyone, was the bow-and-arrow. I had no idea how to handle a bow or fire an arrow, as it was not a skill I really needed to learn back home. In my time, there was no need to hunt for our food. It was more important I could find my way around a computer than a bow. As the group lined up to demonstrate their prowess with the weapon for the first time, I put myself at the end of the line. I closely watched the others as they went through the process of trying to hit a sack of grass barely ten feet away. Most, but not all I noticed, were clearly well used to the weapon and managed to hit the sack or come pretty close.

When it was handed to me, I tried to look as confident as possible. I held up the bow, nocked the arrow, pulled it back, took aim, and let it fly. In any other circumstances, being the first time I had ever fired the weapon, I would have been thought of as doing pretty well. The arrow cut through the air, swirled away to one side, and missed the target by a good four or five feet to be lost in the bushes beyond. The leader came up, having clearly noticed my awkwardness with the weapon, looking at me, wondering perhaps how I could never have learned to fire a bow. He said something directly to me, staring me in the face. Of course, I had no idea what he said. All I could do was shrug my shoulders. Strangely enough, I felt somehow I had let him down. He took the weapon away from me and nodded toward the bushes. I set off to find the arrow.

Chapter Thirteen

I lifted up the basket with the piglet and carried it for New Water. I felt sorry for her, an elderly woman still made to work hard. I was also wondering if perhaps she had lost some of her reasoning in her old age. I could not believe for a moment that, even in the River Settlement, people were allowed to own other people. It was ridiculous. It made no sense whatsoever. How could someone own another person? It was like trying to say a person could own the water tumbling in the river. Both were impossible. I followed her away from the pig sty to an adjacent small lean-to hut.

"Come in," she said, going ahead. "Welcome to my home. It's not much, I guess, but it is mine."

I went in and looked around, taking in the bare essentials of the hut.

"I live here on my own," she said, as if almost admitting a dark secret. "I had a family once, but no more."

"I'm sorry."

Another peculiar aspect of the River Settlement. At the Lake Settlement, a person would never be left to live alone. They would, if even a little grudgingly, be taken in by another family member.

"Come over to the hearth. Take a seat there and warm yourself," she said, pointing to a log stump.

As she poked the fire to bring it back to life, I let the basket down on the earth floor. The heat of the hut was welcome after so long living out in the open air. I sat where she had indicated, opened my hands, and warmed myself. New Water produced bread and, to my great surprise, some pork and grizzled fat in a ceramic bowl.

"One of the advantages of keeping pigs for the chief," she said with a wink. "There is always a little spare going. Are you here on your own?"

"I came with a man. Some of the men took him away this morning."

"For training, probably by the little cub."

"Little cub?"

"Sorry, it's a joke of mine. That's what I call the chief's son. The little cub running around following his father's every wish. Struck Stone is in charge of training new recruits. He is a mean one, but fair in a tough sort of way. You do not have to worry. He will not put your man through anything that he himself would not do."

"How many children does Wolf Killer have?"

I was surprised at the mention of Wolf Killer having a son. I had never envisaged him as a family man. I saw him rather as a lone malicious force.

"Two, Struck Stone is the oldest and then there is Tall Grain. She's about your age, but not half as agreeable. Believe me, she would never get down in the mud to help an old woman. She is far too full of herself. They say she is her father's favorite, probably because they are most alike. The two siblings hate each other and their father is happy to keep them at each other's throats."

"And their mother?"

"Gone to her ancestors while giving birth to Tall Grain. Tell me, where are you staying?"

"On the beach."

"On the beach? That won't do. There will be rain later today. You can stay here tonight if you want. It's warm, at least, and out of the rain. I have a lot to do for the feast. You could help me if you want, while you're waiting for your man. Something to pass the time."

"Yes, I would like that."

"Good, let's start by getting that runt up to the hall."

During the course of the next few days, working alongside New Water as we and others like her prepared for the feast, I saw at firsthand that life for a slave in the River Settlement was a hard one. New Water had little respite from her chores. Even worse, in my opinion, she was treated with no respect by those around her. In the Lake Settlement, the elderly were always, well almost always, given due deference and listened to by the younger members of the settlement. Here, most people seemed to ignore her other than asking short, brisk questions about how soon she would finish whatever particular task she was currently working on. There was one clear advantage to her positon, however, at least for me. She could go almost all over the settlement without raising any suspicions from anyone, including into the inner timber palisade.

I soon found that life there, beyond the palisade, was a mystery. For starters, a number of people lived inside its wooden embrace whose sole task was serving the household of Wolf Killer. They were neither farmers nor hunters, but something new. They were mouths to be fed on the work of others. The food inside the palisade flowed freely from a cooking area located on the inside of the wall near a pond. This area consisted of an always open hut, a butchering ground that buzzed constantly with masses of flies, a large outdoor fire with a stout wooden spit, and several smaller fire pits. The whole bloodied and charcoal mess was presided over by a bad-tempered cook and two of his permanently put down helpers.

It was extraordinary for me to meet people who never worked the land or hunted for their food, but relied on others to provide for their daily meals. I had never met anyone in my entire life who did not personally provide most of the food they consumed. Even my uncle, leader of the Lake Settlement, took full part in working the farms and tending the animals. The idea that the Lake People should support him simply because he was the leader would have been laughed at. Our farmers worked hard, without any outside help, to support their families. Perhaps the only situation I knew that came closest to the notion was our shaman. In addition to her own small flock of sheep she kept up by the Stone House, she was intermittently given extra foodstuffs by those wishing her help in contacting their ancestors to ask for favors.

The people who worked inside the palisade also spent a great deal of their day idly talking about each other and the family of Wolf Killer. Rumors were abounding that Wolf Killer was looking for either a wife for his son or a husband for his daughter. Tonight, a visiting party of another chief was arriving from much farther down the river. People said that Wolf Killer was hoping to make an alliance with him through the marriage. The great feast was in their honor. Wolf Killer had himself personally traveled by boat some of the way down the river to meet the party and escort them back to his settlement.

It was difficult, however, in amidst of all the gossip, to discern what was true and what was false. The talk about Tall Grain, it seemed to me at least, was particularly spiteful at times. Perhaps that was because she was a woman, or simply because everyone seemed afraid of her. She ruled over the palisade with a hard hand. I had seen her for the first time some days ago as she walked along one of the exterior paths with the cook, issuing instructions for the coming feast. She was tall, red-haired, with wide blue eyes.

New Water sank to the wall of the nearest structure at her approach and pulled me back as well. I followed suit as I had no wish to stand out. After all, I really had no right to be there. Although, so far, as I trailed around after New Water and followed her directions, no one had questioned me as to why I was there. Tall Grain had swept past and had not even looked at us.

The preparations for the feast had been ongoing since before I arrived. In the morning, New Water and I tended the pigs and then walked up to the palisade to help where we were needed. There was a lot of work to be done. One of the houses had to be cleaned out and bales of fresh bedding brought in for the guests. The main hall had to be readied and decorated with fresh paint motives. In addition, the foods for the feast were coming in from all over Wolf Killer's domain and had to be slaughtered or stored away. Jugs and jugs of apple cider were brought in and carefully watched over. Wolf Killer wanted to impress his guests, and Tall Grain wanted to impress her father.

As I worked over the past days, I carefully learned the layout of the lodgings and various structures within the palisade. I noted in particular the sleeping quarters of Wolf Killer and the various huts used by the warrior guards.

So far, I had not ventured into any of the buildings, other than the main hall where we were currently working, for fear of getting caught before I had decided on my plan. However, I knew I was running out of time. Wolf Killer was returning. The ancestor could not keep up his pretense forever. I needed to act today.

And yet, even at this stage, I had no idea what my real plan was. Why had I come with the boy thus far? Just to find my father's heart? I did not know, but something, some idea of what I had to do, pulled me on. What was it? Was I really thinking of taking revenge for my father? Was I really thinking of drawing blood, of waiting until Wolf Killer slept after he'd gotten drunk at the feast so I could creep forward with the small knife Crow had given me? I did not know. The plan was at best half formed in my mind. Still, I thought, whatever I decided on, it would be useful to see inside Wolf Killer's lodging. To make myself familiar with the interior layout so I could find my way around it in the dark if I needed to.

The modest structure Wolf Killer used was the highest building inside the palisade. Making an excuse that I needed to go out to the toilet, I left New Water and slipped out of the main hall. I went away along the pathways up to the building. I listened outside for a few moments. Hearing nothing, I pushed in at the door and went through. The interior was a one-roomed space. It was dark inside. In a few moments, my eyes adjusted to the gloom and I moved forward into the center of the room.

It was very basic and almost bare. There was no furniture, only a length of bedding on the ground beside a hearth. The fire was cold now, but it would be lit on Wolf Killer's return. A large woven blanket was spread out on the other side of the hearth. Lying on the blanket was a roll of fur and some weapons. I was very surprised at the state of Wolf Killer's lodging, as I had been expecting something more grandiose as befitting someone of his status. Yet, as I looked around, I was struck by the simplicity of his sleeping quarters. It reminded me of an outdoor campsite that had been brought indoors. It was the home of a man who only rested there, had no need for domesticity, and indeed longed to be out in the wild beyond the palisade.

The blanket by the hearth held my attention. It seemed peculiar that a man such as Wolf Killer, who clearly had no interest in adding any personal touch to his sleeping quarters, would take such care in laying out the various items on the blanket. I knelt and unrolled the fur. It was a grey wolf skin. Was it the original wolf, I wondered, that had given Wolf Killer his name? The weapons beside it were an axe, a spear head, and a bow along with a leather quiver full of arrows. These were special items for Wolf Killer. The presence of the wolf skin showed that they were of great value to him. They probably had a very personal history and meaning for him.

I had seen the same notion many times before where an item was believed to be special, even thought to hold an extraordinary power, and as such was kept as a talisman. Even my father had a stone axe that his father had given him. He never used it, but had kept it high in the rafters of the house for safe keeping. Thinking upon the arrowhead the ancestor boy sought, I picked up the leather quiver and carefully removed each shaft and inspected the attached arrowheads. How each arrowhead was distinctive for Wolf Killer, I could not tell them. They all looked ordinary to me.

Once I had removed all the arrows, I noticed there was a bulge at the bottom of the quiver. Reaching in, I pulled out a small leather cloth that was wrapped up and tied around with grass twine. I laid it on the blanket, undid the twine, and let the cloth flap open to reveal another arrowhead and a rounded lump of meat the size of a man's fist. I was puzzled at first until, suddenly, I realized what the piece of meat was.

I remembered when my father had slaughtered and butchered one of the old sows for the coming winter. I remembered how he had stopped in his work and called me over. He wanted me to see something. He held a plump, droplet-shaped meat portion with small tubes sticking out in his blood-stained hands.

"The heart of the animal," he had said softly. "Where the spirit lives."

I pulled back from the blanket. I knew what I had found. This was my father's heart. Different from that of a pig, but still recognizable. The accompanying arrowhead had to be the weapon that had killed him. My poor father. I knew I could not leave the items here. How would my father ever find his way to his ancestor's Stone House if his heart was in this terrible place? Taking the items meant I would definitely have to act tonight. If Wolf Killer found that his prizes from the attack on my farm were missing, he would order a search of the entire settlement. It would not be long before an accusing finger was pointed at the new girl. I wrapped up the heart alongside the arrowhead in the leather cloth and pushed the pile into my clothing. I returned the arrows to the quiver and rearranged the items on the blanket as I had found them. I went back to the door and stepped out to leave. There was a man there, almost about to come through the doorway, who seemed as surprised as me at our meeting.

"What are you doing here?" he demanded.

"I was told to check the chief's bed," I said, thinking quickly. "The bedding needed changing."

"Where is the old bedding then?" he asked.

"I was only checking. I have not replaced it yet. I have to gather up the new material first. Please, I must get on with my work. My aunt is waiting for me. I need to finish before the chief returns."

"Fine, but next time, tell someone before you go in there. If the chief found you in there, it would not be well for you."

"Yes, thank you."

I hurried down to the hall where everyone was still busy. Some of the men were bringing in a set of log seats that Tall Grain had ordered specially cut for the occasion. She was giving orders to the men to arrange the seats in the correct manner around the now burning central hearth for Wolf Killer and his guests.

I spotted New Water with a group of other women across the hall sorting through a pile of blankets and hides which were to cover the seats for the guests' added comfort.

I walked over to her and smiled.

"Are you all right, my dear?" she asked.

"I'm fine."

"You were gone a long time."

"I'm all right now."

"Are you sick?"

"No, it's just my monthly red womanhood."

She looked as if she was going to ask another question, but was cut short by a commotion at the main door to the hall. A man walked in. I recognized him as the one who had thrown the ancestor into the river on our first morning here. He was followed by two other men who were dragging a fourth unconscious man between them. I looked on in astonishment as they threw the man onto the floor and he rolled over onto his back close to the fire. It was the ancestor.

Chapter Fourteen

I could tell that this evening was going to be different. After a long afternoon of the usual exercises, they took us to the large public fire near the beach instead of back to the field. As one of the women there handed around bowls of stew, I stood next to the fire and let its warmth invade my body. It felt nice.

Some of the other lads started smiling as they tucked into the food with their hands. They thought that being brought to the fire meant their ordeal was over. They believed they had completed their tasks. They believed they had been accepted.

I was not so sure. I could see the leader and his goons talking among themselves and they were not relaxed. We were not brought here as a reward, I sensed, but as a preparation for the coming events. Sure enough, after a short while, the leader gave a command and the woman went around collecting the bowls.

One of the men followed her, handing out axes from a sack. By this stage, I was well used to the axe. I held mine aloft by the wooden handle to feel the weight and posture of the stone head. I noticed that the head was not blunt, as before on all our previous training exercises, but sharpened into a strong diagonal edge.

The leader spoke and we all filed out away from the fire, through the settlement, and into the darkening land beyond. After a while, the leader picked up his stride and broke into a run. I could feel the growing tension between the group, as the rest of the lads caught onto what I had felt earlier, and knew that this was not a normal exercise. Whatever was coming, it was for real this time. No more games. We ran on and on. Those of the original group who would not have been able to keep up with the pace had long since left. Indeed, of the group of lads I had met on the first morning, nearly half had gone. Laughter Dude, Grumpy Git, and most surprising of all, Bread Boy, were still there, but Grounder was gone. None of those who left had been forced out. They all had decided of their own free will to leave, either stepping out to speak to the leader or slipping away when no one was looking.

Truth be told, I was glad they had left and, in some ways, was a little contemptuous of them for leaving. Back home, I would have found it difficult to fit into such a small closed group like this. Now, after training hard together, I felt proud to be part of it and even enjoyed the company of the others. Those that had failed had proven themselves to be weak, and so were not good enough for us. The training had not just been physical, but had involved subtle mental preparation as well. They wanted us to feel, not superior as such, but stronger than the rest.

We stuck to the course of the river for an hour or so until turning away from the water onto the flat plain. We crossed the grass lands, heading for the distant high ground. As the sun was falling below the horizon, we climbed, without even a break in our step, up to the crest of the hill, which was covered in woodland.

We barely slowed on moving through the trees, but kept going until coming out the other side. There, the leader waved a hand and we came to a stop. He crouched down low and went forward. We followed, adopting a similar position. I crept up and stopped at the line. Below us at the foot of the hill, I could see a collection of three houses placed in a rough circle around a central fire area.

Apart from one or two people still walking around, the settlement was empty and I figured most of the inhabitants must have retired to their houses for the night.

I was starting to get a very bad feeling about this. Why were we out in the middle of nowhere spying on what appeared to be an insignificant settlement compared to the one we had left behind? Surely, this tiny cluster of houses, being so close to our own much bigger settlement, must more or less be under its effective control. What had the people here done to get the attention of the River Settlement? I hoped that the leader was not planning to attack it as they had done at Farm Girl's home. In some ways, I had been working so hard at fitting in with them, I had forgotten what type of people they actually were.

The leader held up his hand and flicked one finger to the right, then two fingers to the left before lastly thrusting a closed fist straight ahead. One of his goons tapped the shoulder of the nearest lad. They peeled away and ran down the right side of the hill while another group consisting of the second goon and two other lads went down the left hand side of the hill. The leader watched their progress, and when judging them to have covered sufficient distance, set off directly down the slope with the rest of us following. We approached the settlement in silence and soon reached the nearest house. Again, we broke formation. Some of the boys were directed around the side of the house to the rear while I went with the leader to the front entrance.

I glanced around and saw that all of the houses were similarly being surrounded. The one or two late stragglers still outside were quickly overpowered. Hands grasped their mouths to prevent them giving an alarm.

A dog, finally hearing us, barked inside the house we had encircled, and after a moment, I heard a man talking. A woman responded and then there were some rushed words louder than before so to be heard over the still yelping dog. The door to the house swung open and a man stepped out holding a wooden club. He peered across the settlement. Of course, he never thought to look behind him.

Our leader took two quick silent steps toward him and kicked out hard at the back of the man's knee.

With a shout, the man buckled, fell, and collapsed face first onto the ground. The leader sprung forward and brought the heel of his foot down on the man's hand holding the club. The man struggled to regain his footing, but the leader swung his axe down so the head nuzzled into the back of the man's neck. He said a few words and the man gave up the fight.

More people appeared from the house, including a woman, two children, and an older man. Our leader nodded toward the central fire area of the house cluster. The lads at the rear of the house joined us and herded the people toward the center.

I found myself in front of the older man, who stared up at

me in dire fright. He remained fixed to the spot, and to my shame, I reached out and gave him a shove with the axe handle. Not with a lot of force, but enough to make him move.

He stumbled, but thankfully joined the others. As they were moved on, the leader stepped off the fallen man, who stood slowly and was pushed in to join his people. The other houses were also being searched and the inhabitants brought out.

The crowd of frightened and defenseless people was now enclosed by a ring of young men holding weapons. *This isn't right*, I thought, *this is just plain wrong.* It was like some of the black and white footage I had seen on television where cruel soldiers pushed around weeping people. What was I becoming?

I was sweating. I had to do something, did I not? I could not just stand here and do nothing, but, I had to admit, at the back of my mind was another reprehensible thought—go along with the group or else they might turn on me. I looked around at the other boys. I could see Laughter Dude was not smiling now but holding his axe nervously and glancing from side to side as if also unsure what was happening.

The leader spoke and one of his goons went forward to grab the man the leader had first assaulted. He was pulled away from the group, pushed to his knees, and his head forced down so his neck was exposed.

A small girl yelled out and ran to throw herself onto him, but the goon knocked her away with his free hand. She fell crying to the ground. A woman came forward and took hold of the girl. The kneeing man said a few words, obviously to the crying child, telling her perhaps not to worry as daddy would be all right. The child buried her head in the woman's embrace.

Our leader and the kneeing man spoke for a few moments. I had no idea what they were saying. Clearly, accusations of some type were being laid out and the man was begging for his life. After a few moments, our leader pulled away. He waved his hand in annoyance at the man's answers, indicating the conversation was over.

He walked away from the group and stood staring into the gloom beyond the settlement for a long while. We all waited. He then turned and pointed his axe at me. At first, I did not understand what he meant. I remained standing in my spot. He came forward, took hold of me, and pulled me over to the kneeing man. He held up his own axe and brought it down in a mock swinging motion.

Are you joking? I thought. *Are you joking? You want me to kill him in front of his family?* I looked at the leader and then around at the other people. Everyone was staring at us. None of the other lads made to move. No one was going to help me. The decision was mine alone. I realized at that moment I had to choose what to do. I could go along with his orders and betray everything I believed that I knew about myself, or I could face the consequences like a man.

"No," I said softly.

If the leader noticed the strange word, he did not show it, but seeing my lack of action, he seized my hand and raised my arm high in the air. He held it tight and began to bring my axe down onto the man's neck.

"No," I said, louder this time. I struggled against his hold and managed to pull my arm up again.

He leaned right into me until we were only an inch or so apart and screamed the order. I could smell his breath while his spit fell onto my face.

"No," I shouted. "I won't kill him."

This time, he clearly heard, as did everyone, and he stepped back, releasing my hand. He smiled and nodded at me. I had found my conscience again, but at what cost? This had not been another test, but a trap into which I had fallen. He swung his own axe and brought it around to hit me full on the side of the head. The pain jumped through my skull and I fell to the ground. As my eyes closed, I saw the leader kick the kneeing man so he toppled over onto the dirt. Then the leader turned away.

Chapter Fifteen

The ancestor was bleeding from the side of his head and seemed a little dazed, as if only just waking up. The man who had come into the hall first stretched out his hands to warm himself over the fire.

"Is my father back?" he asked aloud.

"Yes, Struck Stone, he's back." The answer came from Tall Grain, who was staring at her brother across the hall.

"Good, where is he?"

"He is resting after his journey."

"Tell him I have brought him a gift. Tell him that he will want to see this or, at least, hear it."

"And what have you brought him?"

"I have brought the man who attacked my men."

"Really, the mysterious attacker, the one who appeared from nowhere and knocked out one of your men with a single blow?" Tall Grain came forward and looked down with genuine interest at the ancestor, who was coming around more fully and trying to push himself up onto his elbows.

"Are you sure?" she asked. "He does not look very...fierce. He looks very common to me. The same as any of the other farm boys you want to turn into warriors."

"It is him," Struck Stone said. "He is not the same as the rest. Believe me, I knew he was not the same. He had no idea how to handle a weapon correctly. He moves differently. He does not understand our words, and what he says is..."

"Is what, brother?"

"Different."

"Different," Tall Grain repeated the word.

"Yes."

"You seem delighted with yourself."

"Don't be jealous, Tall Grain."

"Jealous of you? No, you are still a little boy bringing

home silly gifts hoping to please your father."

"Say whatever you want. Father will be happy. This man is trouble. We all know that. Knocking out a Wolf Man, stopping the attack, and challenging our power. People were talking about him and now we have him. The problem is solved."

"Are you absolutely certain, though, he is the same man? Are you not simply trying to make up for your men's failures at the farm? After all, their instructions were simple enough. Burn the farm and kill everyone. So simple, you didn't even bother going with them. That does seem like a terrible mistake now, of course. The farmer's family got away and your men were attacked by the Forest People."

"You are just annoyed that, on the night of your great feast, I have brought a gift that Father will want more than all your hard work. Poor Tall Grain, you really think you will be the next leader here. I control the warriors, so when our father is gone, I shall rule here. Remember who you will answer to then."

"My stupid big brother," Tall Grain said with a smile. "What do you think I do when you are out burning down houses? Look around you. The people inside the palisade are loyal to me. I already own the River Settlement. When Father is gone, I shall answer to no one."

"When father is gone." A low voice growled from a shadowy group of figures who had entered unseen from the side entrance to the hall. "My children, it seems, are all very eager for me to join my ancestors."

I turned in astonishment at the voice. A man, tall and broad with a bearded face, walked forward into the center of the hall. It was Wolf Killer. The man who had brought about the death of my father, shattered my mother, and destroyed my home. I felt my stomach heave on seeing him and a surge of anger flooded through me.

"This is the man who interfered with the attack on the farm?" he asked, coming forward to examine the ancestor, who by now was slowly getting to his feet.

"Yes," Struck Stone said.

"How can you tell?"

"Make him talk."

Wolf Killer reached out and struck the boy hard on the face. He stumbled back but remained quiet.

"He does not want to talk," Wolf Killer said.

"Put his face to the fire," Struck Stone commanded the men standing behind the ancestor.

They seized the ancestor by his arms and pushed him down toward the hearth. He wriggled under their firm grip, but they forced him closer and closer to the heat.

I had to do something. I dropped the blanket I had been holding and slipped a hand under my clothing around the handle of my flint blade. I began slowly, unnoticed, to make my way around the fire toward Wolf Killer, who was watching his son's work. Finally, before they actually shoved his face into the flames, and obviously not realizing that they wanted to hear him speak, the ancestor let out a roar of strange, un-known words.

The people in the hall gasped while Struck Stone looked very pleased.

"Where was he found?" Wolf Killer asked.

"We did not find him," Struck Stone said. "He came to us."

"Really?"

"Yes, to train as a warrior."

"He came to us," Wolf Killer repeated.

I moved farther around the fire. No one paid any heed to me. All eyes were firmly on the three men. I was coming at Wolf Killer from his side while he was looking ahead. I was now within striking distance. I would never get another chance like this. I had probably gotten closer than any assas-sin ever had before. His neck was exposed and open. I pulled the knife up out of my clothing. All I had to do was cover the last short distance, swing the knife back and plunge the hard flint into his skin. My father and home would be avenged. They would almost certainly strike me and the boy down in the moments afterward, but I would have my revenge. My hand was shaking. Could I do it, though? Would my revenge be worth the cost? Was I a killer?

"And how," Wolf Killer said, "could a man who does not even speak our words get into our home so easily?"

"Father?" Struck Stone asked.

"Somebody must have helped him," Wolf Killer pointed out.

"Her," another voice said.

I turned at the voice and saw Boar step from the half-hidden party of men who had accompanied Wolf Killer into the hall. He was pointing directly at me.

Wolf Killer spun around, spotted me and the weapon in my hand. He moved fast, too fast for a man his size, and stepped across the distance between us. In one swift action, he took hold of my hand carrying the knife and, using that hand as leverage, pulled me around while his other arm wrapped around my neck.

I felt his beard bristle against my cheek and could smell his warm stale breath. At that moment, it seemed as if we were the only two people in the hall. The rest of the Wolf People, the ancestor struggling with the men holding him, the indecision of Struck Stone, and the look of frustration on Tall Grain's face now that I had been stopped in my assassination attempt, all faded away.

"Good girl," Wolf Killer whispered in my ear. "You're braver than my own children."

He picked the knife from my grasp before flinging me casually to the ground.

"In my absence, my home has, it seems, become over-run with enemies," he said. "Where are you from? Who sent you?"

I remained quiet, glaring up at him. Wolf Killer walked over to the ancestor and held my own blade up to his jugular.

"Who sent you?"

"No one sent her," Boar said. "She came on her own. She is called Wild Flower. No one tells her what to do."

"You're the girl who escaped from the farm," Wolf Killer guessed. "The man killed there was your father?"

"Yes." I wanted him to know the truth and the pain he had made me suffer.

"So you are from the Lake Settlement? They sent you to kill me."

"No, that's not it..."

"She is," Boar said. "Her uncle is leader there."

"I am surprised," Wolf Killer said. "My spy in the Lake Settlement told me attacking that farm would bring the Lake People to their senses. They would submit to me without a fight after that. I was told the Lake People were weak and frightened. I see they have decided on another path. I thought I had made my point clear enough, obviously not."

"You killed my father to make a point?"

"You probably don't realize it, but your settlement is important, very important. Your lake controls the other side of the mountain. It controls the river and access to all the land beyond. When I rule the Lake Settlement, I will send my men down the river to take all the settlements along it. Perhaps I can get as far as the Wide Water they say is on the other side of the land."

"You have no right to go anywhere near the Lake Settlement," I said. "That land is ours, our fathers and their fathers lived there."

"This is not about the past. It is about the future. The forest is vanishing while the land is filling up more and more every year. We cannot go on as before, when our ancestors first came to this land. We are no longer living in isolated settlements separated by mountains and rivers. We are now becoming one people, interlinked with one another. I will unite all the settlements. Together, we will all be stronger. Then, we will have peace and prosperity for everyone."

"Peace? All you really want is more land to seize, more men as your killers. You can never have peace, not a man like you. Peace? You're just a greedy warmonger."

His composure dropped just for a moment—he flashed a look of open annoyance at me—until his appearance of calm leadership returned.

"The Lake Settlement will submit like everyone else. I had hoped you would give in without any trouble. I see I will have to take a more direct approach." He looked away from me and turned with arms raised to smile at the crowd around him. "But now, we have a feast to get ready for and guests who need to be pampered. Struck Stone, take these two out past the palisade and kill them. I don't want any blood messing up the hall your sister has spent so long preparing."

Struck Stone came toward me, but stopped when a shower of red sparks fell from above onto his shoulders. He batted them away with his hand. At first, I thought that the hearth fire had burst awake with a crackling of wood and sent a billow of sparks into the air to float down again. I looked up, though, and saw a dull orange glow spreading among the roof thatch above me. A long time ago, when I was young and we still lived in the Lake Settlement, I had been in a house fire. I could not remember who owned the house and why we were staying there. I only remembered being woken from my sleep and the house being full of dense smoke. It had been a terrifying experience as my father bundled me into his arms to escape the blaze all around us. I still had a vivid memory of being squeezed tight as he ran through the heat. Now, the experience helped me as I grasped what was happening quicker than the others in the hall and so was able to react faster.

As shouts broke out amid the growing smoke, I took the ancestor's hand and pulled him away from the now alarmed men and set off at a run to the main entranceway. I looked around for New Water to tell her to get out, but I could not see her anywhere in the hall. I knew that it was vital to get out quickly. The fire would spread rapidly along the roof, especially as the underside of the thatch had been dried out night after night by the internal hearth. The fire, smoke, and panic could not be fought. The only option was to run. Ahead of us, a section of the flaming roof collapsed to the floor, hitting a screaming man. We skirted around it, waving the heat and sparks away with our hands, and kept running.

By now, others were turning for the entranceway, but we were just ahead of them by a fraction and managed to pass through out into night beyond before the doorway became clogged with terrified people.

We did not stop but hurried away quickly. Only at a safe distance did I turn and look. Behind us, the flames on the roof were reaching up into the sky. A mob of people was rushing around with whatever containers they could find to fill with water from the kitchen pond. The goal, as always in cases of fire, was not to stop the flames overwhelming the structure that was burning, which after all could be rebuilt, but to stop the flames from spreading out. A fire that got out of control could scorch rapidly through an entire settlement. As I watched, Wolf Killer burst through the people crammed into the entrance, pushing those in front of him to the ground.

We set off away from the crowd, heading toward the palisade gateway where I spotted New Water waiting by the one of the pillars watching the fire anxiously above her on the crest of the rise. The only way she could have gotten out so quickly was if she had started the fire herself.

"Thank you, New Water," I said.

"As if I would let those cubs harm you. You remind me of my own daughter too much," she said, handing over a sack. "Take this and go quickly, whoever you are."

"Come with us."

"Not at my age. Just go."

"Thank you again. May you see your daughter at the Stone House of your ancestors."

"Goodbye."

We went past the gate and out through the settlement. We had to get away for our own safety, but also to warn the Lake Settlement. Wolf Killer was not finished with the Lake Settlement. Indeed, the Wolf People would undoubtedly see the burning of his hall as an attack by the Lake People. He burnt one of our houses, my farm, so we came to burn his. He could not let the war challenge go unanswered. He would have to respond with a strong and blunt fist to maintain his own standing and reputation. He would come for the Lake Settlement very soon. And who was telling him of events in the Lake Settlement? Who was the traitor there?

A light drizzle fell. It would help with the fire. I did not know if I was happy or annoyed at that, but on the other hand, it would help cover our tracks a little. Still, a good tracker like Boar would be able to follow us easily. He must have fled in the direction of the River Settlement after his failed assassination attempt on the ancestor. Why had Crow not found and dealt with him as he promised? As we left the River Settlement behind us, I had no idea which way to go. I stopped and looked around. Every way seemed equally dangerous, but we had to get going. I started moving the way we were facing when the boy pulled my arm and instead pointed in another direction.

Chapter Sixteen

We were nearly at the marsh when they found us. I knew that getting to the wetlands was our best hope of getting away from the men who were surely following us. They did not strike me as the sort of men who let an enemy escape. The fire had given us some time, but we had to be quick. I had seen myself how they could track a man in a game of chase. It did not take much to appreciate that the same skills could be applied to hunting us for real. If we tried to escape on the river or any other direction overland from the settlement, they would easily catch up with us. I had, however, witnessed the impact of the marshes on the lads I trained with, how deeply frightened they had been of the sodden terrain, and figured that if we ventured into its depths, they might not follow us in. We at least would have a decent chance.

As we reached the summit of the hill overlooking the marsh, I turned and scanned the ground falling away behind us. By the light of the rising moon, I could see a party of dim shapes silently coming up toward us. I took the girl's hand, and together we sprinted over the hill top and straight into the descent on the other side. I heard her let out a barely audible gasp of alarm when she saw the marshland spread out below us.

We were moving so fast down the hill I lost my footing and fell head-over-heel to tumble a few feet through the thorny scrub. I got up and looked behind me. Sure enough, there on the slope above us, I could see the outline of the chasing men.

"Come on." I shouted more to myself than to her.

We reached the bottom of the hill where the dry ground seeped into the soggy wash. We pushed on, without pausing, and the water got deeper and deeper. I felt the freezing cold bite into my feet. It was heavy going. The water eventually went up to my knees and became as thick as soup. Even with the light of the moon, it was difficult to find a path. Finally, I climbed up onto a streak of drier grass. I looked over my shoulder to where the girl was following me without a word. Even though we had only spent such a short time together previously, it was good to see her again.

During my training, when I was being tested day after day, I had thought about her a lot and, funny as it was, I had found myself missing her. It was ridiculous. We did not even speak the same language, but still I missed her voice and being around her. I was surprised to see her in the hall, even more surprised when she lunged with her knife at that man. It did not take much to realize he had probably been involved in the death of her father. I was not sure about her actions, of trying to kill a man like that, but this was a strange place. Perhaps, in the absence of prisons and court systems, that was how justice was carried out? It still seemed wrong.

My heart had nearly stopped when I saw the man grab her. I tried to help but was unable to break free of my captors. And then the fire had started. Obviously, it could not be a coincidence. Someone, the old lady by the gate maybe, had set the fire to help us escape.

I peered back and saw that the men following had come down the hill. They were staring out over the marsh at us. The leader who had trained me and then tried to burn me had advanced a short distance into the water. He turned to the others, still up on the higher ground, and shouted something at them, but they refused to move. He cried out in disgust and pushed forward a few more feet, but he moved so slowly and cautiously that I knew he would never catch up with us. I could tell he badly wanted to reach us, but even he, brave and strong as he was, could not overcome a lifelong fear of the marshlands.

I turned away from them and set about picking out a path as best I could. I stayed away from the mournful water on either side of us and instead keep to the high patches of dry ground. That meant, of course, that we weaved a meandering trail through the marsh. The hill behind us grew smaller as we went farther and farther in. Even if they decided to try again in the morning, in the full glare of daylight when it might have been easier for them to conquer their fears, the watery maze of trees and dry patches would effectively hide our movement. The moon gleamed down, and it offered a sort of reassurance to me. It was still there, despite all that had happened. The moon remained shining. The same now as it was in my day, always looking out over the actions, both good and bad, of mankind.

I then heard the girl shriek behind me and stumble headlong to grab my hand. I feared that the men from the settlement were somehow upon us. I spun around and saw she was pointing out to the far distance on one side where small balls of light hovered over the water. At first, I thought they were torches being held by men closing in on us from another angle. Then, after a few seconds, I saw that the lights were not moving, as would be expected if they denoted men coming toward us, but rather bobbed gently up and down in the same position. I was not sure what I was looking at until, in a flash of insight, I recognized them. They were Will-o'-the-Wisps. I had never actually seen one in real life before. I only knew them from books and Saturday morning cartoons on television when I was a kid.

She held my hand tight and appeared genuinely frightened by their appearance. I supposed in her culture they must have believed that the lights were living things that inhabited the marshes. Judging by her reaction, they were not considered friendly.

That would explain why they were all so reluctant to enter the marsh if they believed there was some type of malicious creature living out here. I guessed when people got lost in the marsh, which no matter how much they avoided the area must have happened occasionally in bad weather, and fell into one of the deep pools to be drowned, they blamed what they thought to be the fire creatures. I vaguely remembered that Will-o'-the-Wisps were caused by gases being released from the rotten material below the surface, which, somehow or other, then combusted to give off the strange dancing flames. Was that it? I was not sure, but I did know they were a natural occurrence. At least that was what I rationally told myself. Out here, though, alone in the middle of a vastness of still water and tormented trees, I could understand her feelings of dread. They were a natural event that seemed to portray a supernatural element. I moved on and she turned away, glad it seemed to have been pulled away from the enticing fairy lights.

We went on through the night, to put as much distance between us and our pursuers as possible. As morning approached, evident by the first thin glimmer of pale light on the horizon, I knew that exhaustion was overtaking me. I had not had a proper night's sleep in ages and it was catching up with me. I faced her and brought my two hands, palms together, up to my cheek. She seemed to understand the signal for sleep and nodded. I looked for some dry area that would be suitable for the two of us to lie out on. There was nothing around us but the thin patches of scrub and grass. In the distance, though, I spotted a large tree that rose up out of the water before turning on itself and plunging down into the dark liquid murkiness again. Maybe there was space enough there for both of us to rest?

We waded through the water to the tree. One side of the branches was lower than the other and strapped in against the trunk, forming a loose wooden platform. I pulled myself up and then helped her. The space was small but comfortable enough. Of course, our leggings were still wet, but there was little we could do about that. We would not be able to stay there too long with wet clothes, but we had to take a break even for a while.

I hunkered down with my back against the trunk and she followed, resting her head on my chest. Despite the odd location and the circumstances surrounding how we had gotten there, I could not help but feel a little awkward having her so close to me. Without the sound of the water splashing as we walked, the marsh beyond seemed to come alive with the buzz of insects and the croaking of far-off frogs. It was a gentle hum, compared to the intense activity of the last few days, and I found myself relaxing a little.

Back home, I never had the time or, if I was honest, the inclination to spend any time out in the natural world. Perhaps I should have as it seemed I was missing out on something quite beautiful.

She then startled up as if remembering something. She reached down into her clothing and pulled out what seemed to be a ball of leather. She placed it on my stomach, unwrapped the ball, and laid the contents out. I was a little puzzled at first as it only seemed to contain a lump of uncooked bruised meat, which was clearly not for eating, and a single arrowhead. Correction, looking closer, I then realized it was *the* arrowhead. The exact same arrowhead as from my grandad's house. A piece of white flint with the black lightning strike running down its heart. I looked at it in amazement. How had she managed to find it? I simply could not guess.

All I had to do to get home was touch the arrowhead. One movement to go back to my safe and warm existence where people who loved me waited with abundant food and drink. Where I could shower, change, check my phone, and in the evening, go out to meet my friends. One simple action to leave behind this cold, damp, and fear-filled place. To forget about these people who were so prone to violence.

I looked at the girl beside me. Of course, I would also have to leave her alone in the middle of the marshland. To go where and do what I did not know, but effectively abandoning her to deal with those terrible people on her own. That I could not do. I simply could not treat her like that. Why? Was I falling for her or was it a simple human desire not to see our friends hurt? I did not know, but, either way, I could not leave her here. So, instead of touching the arrowhead, I reached out and closed her hand so the leather ball was wrapped up again.

She nodded, accepting my decision, although probably not really understanding it. Instead, she opened the sack that the old woman had given her and pulled out some streaks of cured ham wrapped in leaves. I took a bite. It was, without doubt, the best tasting food I ever had.

Chapter Seventeen

We left the swamp the next day. I was glad to leave behind its rotten stench, icy waters, and the little fiery beasts
that lived there to prey on lost travelers. I was sure they
were coming for us last night to drag us down into the water.

The ancestor had seemed remarkably unbothered by
their appearance. Perhaps they did not have them wherever
he came from. After the swamp, we walked on and on for a
number of days. I did not recognize any of the places or natural landmarks we passed, but using the positioning of Yellow Face, when she wakened and went to sleep, I was able
to roughly work out the direction we needed to travel.

Along the way, we ate the pork strips and bread New
Water had given me and drank from the streams we crossed
over. We slept wherever we were when night came. On the
third or fourth day, we saw the familiar mountain by the
Lake Settlement loom up in the distance. We were getting
closer to home.

That night, we came upon an abandoned encampment
beside a stream. I did not know if it belonged to the Lake
People from past days or was even more ancient than that.
The campsite was a large oval-shaped area formed by a low
earth bank and outer ditch. The site seemed to have been
occupied on successive occasions as evident by the number
of hearths inside the bank. These were marked out by small
stone circles or as lumps of thick, overgrown grass. Back
when my father had been young, or so he told me, the Lake
People had ranged far over the land surrounding their settlement. Back then, they had often used campsites like this
one for fishing, gathering seasonal foods, or trading with distant settlements for rare items such as quality flint pieces.

I felt reassured by the presence of the old campsite and
the thoughts of those who had occupied it previously. As if it

denoted a point of safety in an otherwise wild and dangerous landscape. We settled down for the night. I lit another fire to add to the collection already there.

As we ate the last of the pig meat, the boy reached out and laid a hand on my arm. He nodded over to a patch of grassland, brightened by the last rays of evening sunlight, down by the waterside. A vixen and her three cubs were playing there, having not noticed our arrival. The cubs jumped around the mother fox while she yawned and rested. It gladdened my heart to watch and reminded me that beauty still existed even in these hard days. I slept that night with the warmth of the fire on my face and the solid encampment bank at my back. Tomorrow, we returned to the Lake Settlement. This time, my uncle would find it much harder to keep me quiet.

Despite our hardships, on reaching the settlement, I had no expectation of receiving a warm reception. I was right. The Lake People stopped in their daily routines and stared as we walked into the settlement. As if they knew what our arrival meant. As if they knew who was doubtless following, snapping at our heels. The wolves were coming. My uncle saw us and approached.

"Wild Flower," he said sadly. "What will happen to us now?"

"You decide your own future."

"No, our future will be decided by others."

"If you let them."

"Rumors are spreading like a summer fire through the dry trees. Crow came down here yesterday to tell us everything. The Forest People received a messenger from one of their own, the man called Boar who was here in our own very settlement. He is with Wolf Killer right now."

"I know," I said. "I saw the traitor there myself."

"You were there then?"

"Yes."

"In the land of the Wolf People."

"Yes."

"So, it is true, Crow told us what you did. The hall of Wolf Killer burnt down. Now, he is calling his warriors in from all over his domain. They are gathering around him like a summer storm. Boar said that Wolf Killer is coming here and nothing can stop him."

"Wolf Killer was coming sooner or later," I replied. "He said so himself. The attack on my father's farm was meant to frighten us. He was never going to leave us alone."

"Perhaps, perhaps, I don't know anymore. I am tired, Wild Flower. We have never had to face a threat like this before. Our fathers and their fathers were able to live in peace. The world was bigger then. No one needed to control anyone. We were all free. The land is changing for the worst. Boar said the Forest People must give in to Wolf Killer. I think we should do the same."

I looked around at the downcast people who had gathered about us to listen to my uncle's laments. They did not need to hear his fears. They did not need to hear that I reckoned my uncle a coward or that I had wondered for some days now if his advisor, First Calf, was a spy for the enemy. They did not need to hear accusations or doubt. They needed to be told who they really were.

"My uncle is right," I said in a louder voice. "Our ancestors were free, and I tell you that we still are. It is true that our fathers and grandfathers never faced anything like we now have to, but I tell you, if they had, they would not have given in. They cleared this land and made it their own. They handed it on to us and we have a sacred right to it. Along with that right, comes an obligation. We have a duty to protect the land, so in turn we can hand it on to our children and grandchildren. Then in time, when we have joined our ancestors in the Stone House, when our descendants talk of us, they will do so in awe. They will say that when we faced this threat, we did not submit and we did not back down. We held the ground."

"But how can we defeat Wolf Killer?" First Calf demanded, pushing his way to the front of the crowd. "He is too strong."

"Do you know who burnt down the hall of the Wolf People?" I asked. "It wasn't me, and it wasn't a great warrior or band of men. It was an old woman, a pig farmer in the River Settlement, who burnt his hall. Wolf Killer is only a man. I have seen him. He has the same strengths and weaknesses as each of us here."

"Can't the boy save us, as you claim he saved you?" First Calf asked.

"No, the ancestor is brave, very brave, but he is only a man."

If First Calf was hoping to bully me or drag the crowd along with his wishful thinking, like he did before in my uncle's house, he was sorely mistaken this time. Now, I could see the path I needed to take to ensure the safety of the Lake Settlement. First Calf would not stand in my way. I would listen to each of his notions and dismiss every one of them in a calm, detached manner.

"But we cannot defeat Wolf Killer," he said. "We are so few compared to the Wolf People."

"We will not fight alone. I will travel up to the forest, and I bring Crow and his men down here."

"Fight with the Forest People?" First Calf asked in amazement. "They have probably already joined with Wolf Killer against us."

"No, Crow is a good man. He would not hand over his people to a man like Wolf Killer. He would not abandon his trees or his ancestors. If I know him, he is already making a plan. He will help us. We will be stronger together. But we must start to prepare now. Wolf Killer will need time to gather his men, but the days are passing. We must be prepared for him. Uncle, you must get ready."

"I don't know, Wild Flower," my uncle said. "Maybe First Calf is right. I don't know. Maybe we don't have to surrender to Wolf Killer like you say, maybe we can abandon the settlement, move to another place beyond his reach."

A murmur went up from the crowd at the notion of leaving their homes. I went forward to my uncle and gently took his hand.

"There is nowhere to go. This is our home. The Stone House of our ancestors lies on the hill. Will we abandon those we have left there, our mothers, our fathers and even some of our children? And what of our crops? The grain is ripening and the cattle have their little ones now. Are we to leave all that, go out into the land to see our old ones falter and children cry with the hunger?"

A few in the crowd expressed words of agreement with me. I knew that these were good, strong, and brave folk. They just needed someone to point them in the right direction. My uncle was already defeated, I could see that. I would, if need be, lead these people myself.

"But what should we do then?" my uncle asked, looking pleadingly at me.

"Uncle, rest for a while. I will see to the Lake Settlement."

"You," First Calf exploded, sensing the sudden and unexpected shift in the politics of the settlement and knowing that if my uncle relinquished power, then he too would lose access to that power.

"I will lead for the moment," I said, turning to him. "You can rest along with my uncle or, you can help me, First Calf, to defend our home."

"Help you," he said, clearly weighing up the options open to him.

"Help me," I reiterated, knowing that, even if he was the spy, for the moment it would be an easier transfer of leadership if he went along with it. "There is much to do. We must gather up the children, the old, and those who cannot fight. We have to pack food and clothes for them. They will head down the river. They can make camp there until it is safe to return. The rest of us must prepare to fight. We need to gather up all the weapons we have, and every man and woman of fighting age needs to be armed. We will also need every arrow we can find. We have to send out runners, in pairs, to look for the arrival of any Wolf Men."

The crowd remained still, unsure of what to do.

"And we need to do it now," I said softly but with edge.

"Well, get started, everyone," First Calf shouted, having obviously decided it was time to work with the new leader of the Lake Settlement.

Crow was tired like my uncle. I could see it in his eyes. He was exhausted, but he was not defeated. He had come down to the edge of the forest to meet me and that was indication enough that he was not ready to give in just yet. The knee-high grass around me was damp after a light rain as he walked out from the tree line to stand on the rise of the slope above me.

"You look terrible," he said.

"Thanks."

"I guess burning down settlements and trying to kill people doesn't really agree with you."

"No, how is my mother?"

"She is well. She seems quite content in the forest. She has even begun to adopt some of our ways. You met Boar?"

"Yes, he was there."

"He is no longer one of the Forest People. He has left us to pursue his own selfish ends. I am ashamed of him."

"You said you would find him?"

"We searched the forest, but he got away. He was one of our best trackers, so equally he could hide himself when he wanted. He had a good head start from the Lake Settlement even before we had left. And he knew exactly where he was going."

"Maybe some of your people helped him?"

"No," he said a little too defensively. "He acted alone."

"Fine," I said, deciding that nothing would be gained from pressing the matter too deeply at that moment. "As you said, he has joined his axe with the enemy and become one of them. He is lost."

"And your people, what will they do now?" he asked, accepting the change in tone.

"We stay and fight. We cannot retreat. There is nowhere else to go."

"I thought you would say that."

"And your people?"

"They look to me. It is true, a few, mainly the younger ones, talk about joining with Boar. They want the life they believe he now enjoys. I don't think they fully realize what that means, giving up everything, our land and way of life. I might have some problems with one or two of them, but they will follow me in the end."

"And you? What do you think? You know the Wolf Men will come through your forest to get to us. Do you think they will then go home and leave you in peace? You killed one of their own, remember?"

"I haven't forgotten," he said.

"So?"

"I want to fight, I really do, but..."

"Then it is simple." I interrupted him. "Fight, defend your home by defending ours. You are too small to defend the whole forest. They will spread out and attack like wolves against scattered prey, but here at the Lake Settlement, if we join our forces and come together, we will be a rock against their fangs."

"So we die defending your home instead of ours?" he asked.

"If one of us falls, then the other falls. If one survives, then the other survives. In the end, Wolf Killer will not distinguish between your people and my people."

"And afterward, even if we win, then what?"

"What do you mean?" I asked.

"For my people? I hear of trouble from other bands of Forest People. I hear stories from throughout the forest all along the coast. Every summer more and more farmers come from the Wide Water looking for land. Even if we can win here, even if that was possible against the host of Wolf Men, then what? Will the farmers stop coming every season to cut our trees? Will my beautiful forest grow smaller and smaller, until I have only one tree left to shelter under?"

So, I had been right, the worries of the future weighed on Crow. He saw the coming times but was unable to find a solution to the trouble ahead.

"Crow, I cannot answer that. Only you and your people can face their own future, but here and now, if Wolf Killer is not stopped, I can guarantee that you will not see another season in your forest. Afterward, if you wish, you are always more than welcome to join with the Lake Settlement."

"Join with your people?"

"Yes."

"And you, Wild Flower?"

"Me?"

"You. Who would you join with?"

"I don't understand?"

"In the forest, after the Wolf Men attacked your farm, when I found you in the hole by the tree, I did not come looking to find the strange boy like I said. I came to make sure that you were all right. I was worried about you, and after this, if we have not joined our ancestors, I would like to continue worrying about you."

I looked at him and knew what he was really asking. Would I become his wife? I was surprised by the directness of his question, although, I would say, a little thrilled. Maybe it was the uncertain times, and the threat we all now faced that concentrated his mind and brought the idea to the fore. I guess I had always known, at the back of my thoughts, that Crow liked me but had never really laid bare the notion. Perhaps that was why he had always come down personally to trade with my father rather than sending one of his men? Had all his efforts really been to see me? That would also explain why he had wanted me to have the knife back at the Lake Settlement.

As I thought on it, I wondered if my mother had also noticed his interest in me. I remembered on one of our walks down by the river to gather water, it seemed such a long time ago at this stage, she had asked me if I would like to marry. As my red womanhood had come, this was the time that girls my age would often start to think about marriage. About acquiring a husband, if they wanted one. I was raised on a farm, where animals had to produce offspring every year to ensure our survival, so I had always known from a young age how nature worked. My mother had said I could find a man in the Lake Settlement or, she continued, I could always look among the Forest People. Marriage between one of the Forest People and one of the Lake People was rare but not unheard off. At the time, I thought my mother was only thinking out loud. I did not really grasp what she had meant until now. Had she been referring to Crow in particular? Had she thought him a suitable partner for me?

It was true I had known Crow, more or less, for years. However, at this moment, everything seemed to be thornier than before. What of the ancestor? In the last few days, we had spent so much time with each other I felt that there was a connection born through our shared experiences. I felt we had come to understand one another. But it was more than just that. I had personally seen him to be brave, strong, and, perhaps most important of all, loyal. I greatly admired those qualities. I was sure Crow also possessed such qualities, but I had never spent enough time with him to see them blossom. And was there something else, was I simply more attracted to the ancestor boy, with his own strange ways, than Crow? To be honest, I was very confused, but did not wish to show that to Crow. I simply did not know what I wanted at that moment.

"Now is not the time," I said. "We have a fight to win."

Chapter Eighteen

Farm Girl stood in front of her people and it was not hard to guess what she was saying even if I did not understand a word. Trouble was coming and they had better be prepared. I was exhausted after the events of the last few days and the trek back to her settlement. I wanted nothing more than to rest, but I remained standing with her.

She then vanished in the afternoon so I was left to my own devices. I ate, drank, and warmed myself by one of the exterior fires. As the sun set, I was brought to the same hut where the idiot had tried to kill me previously, but I was so tired any bed would have done. I slept soundly for the rest of the night.

I woke, hungry and thirsty, and went out into the settlement.

Farm Girl was back again, along with that Bird Guy from the woods, and she held up a hand in greeting to me.

I felt a little irritated seeing the two of them talking together so closely. After all, I could not even speak to her. I did not want to hang around gawking at them so, after a breakfast of bread and water, I wandered around the settlement.

It was a busy place that morning. A small crowd of old people were trying to supervise a gaggle of children while sacks were being loaded up with bedding and food. I guessed they were fleeing the approaching fight. That would make sense. The rest of the settlement was staying and preparing for war. I supposed the handy thing about being a farmer in this period was that most of the tools they used in their daily chores could, with a few modifications or even a change in grip, be turned into weapons. Some of the adults were individually trying to show their older children how to hold and use various weapons while other children were on their own playing at being fighters. A group of men had also started a central collection of every spare arrow they could find. At the same time, the carpenters among them were busy making as many new shafts as they could. I noticed that a lot of the shafts were missing flint heads. Rather, they were simply being made into sharpened fire-hardened points probably reflecting the absence of a ready supply of flint arrowheads. They would not be as fatal as a flint head, but would still halt the enemy.

In some ways, I was better prepared than they were for what was coming as I had been in the enemy camp and had trained with them. I stopped to look at one girl standing away from the others. She could not have been more than fourteen. She was holding an axe and attempting to take a swing through the air. She was holding it wrong. I could tell that even from a distance. She was more in danger of slicing open her thigh than hitting any potential enemy. After a few more moments of watching her getting it wrong, I went over, took her hand, changed the positon of the axe, nudged her feet into a better standing point, and moved her arm in the correct downward motion.

She was surprised at my intrusion, but once she saw how much her swing had improved, she smiled. I repeated the action several more times until stepping back to see her technique again. I pointed out, without words, where she still needed improvement and rolled my hand indicating she should try once more.

A few of the other young people had gathered around my demonstration and one of the boys then stepped forward holding his axe. I showed him how to handle it in the proper manner.

I figured these people were not as warlike as those by the river and were not as trained in weapons. They were probably more used to employing their axes for chopping firewood than opening skulls.

Another girl gestured that she wanted help so, in order to save time, I drew a line in the dirt with my foot and signaled that they should all stand at the line. I then spent the rest of the morning going through the motions, demonstrating the precise methods of holding different weapons and correcting them where needed. At one point, I saw that Farm Girl, thankfully no longer talking to the Bird Guy, had stopped in her own work of directing various activities throughout the settlement to watch us in training. She looked on for a few moments before turning back to talk to another man beside her.

I admired her for her leadership of these people and for the way they set about defending their home. I wondered, though, what was I going to do? I was happy to help in their training, but was I really prepared to fight with them? At home, I was still considered just a teenager, by my dad especially, with no responsibilities other than my homework and set household chores given to me to specifically teach me about "responsibility." I could not vote or drive or do anything an adult could do. But here, there were teenagers, male and female, some younger and smaller than me, getting ready to fight.

In all the wars I had learned about in school, men and women my age had fought and, in a lot of cases, died for their ideals. However, even forgetting about my age for the moment, this was still not my home and this was not necessarily my fight. They were willing to die for their home, but why should I? I still had so much to do. I wanted to travel, finish my education, and see life in all its brightness. I had, in addition, returned the girl to her home and could, with head held high, now leave. Could I not?

And yet, I felt that leaving would be a mistake. Was I running out before the job was done? Did I not have to stay to see it through to the end? What, though, would I be fighting for? It then struck me, the coming fight was important not for the people around me and not even necessarily for Farm Girl, but for me myself. Surely, I had to stand my ground or else I would spend the rest of my days regretting it. This was too significant a moment, too full of potential, too full of that life I wished to lead, to simply ignore it. This would be a defining point in my life and I could not, for my own sake, walk away from it. It seemed important because it was important.

Toward the afternoon, a large group of the people from the woods arrived to set up a makeshift camp inside the settlement between the houses. I finished the training session as the youngsters were too then excited to continue. I wandered over with them to watch the woods people. I spotted the White Feather Girl among the rest working away. She was carrying some animal hides, which were being laid over one of the half-globe frames of timber branches they had quickly built.

After the time I had spent here, I could now clearly see the differences between the woods people and those in the settlement around me. They were all more or less identical looking it was true, but they dressed in their own unique clothes with distinct haircuts and dissimilar body ornaments. Moreover, the two groups seemed to carry themselves differently. The ones from the settlement moved with heavy steps as if rooted to the ground while the people from the woods prowled like large predators displaying confidence and strong outward self-awareness with every step.

It came to me that both these sets of people mingled here together, the farmers and the forest hunter-gatherers, were probably in varying degrees the ancestors of the folk back home. Taking into account another six millennia of invasions and migrations, of course. I wondered if any of them were *my* direct ancestors? Now, that would be strange.

The White Feather Girl looked up and saw me watching her. I was mortified that she had seen me and, in order to hide my embarrassment, I waved at her. She waved in reply and I nodded before turning away. I had made enough of a fool of myself for one day. I left their camp and returned to the center of the settlement where they were beginning what could only be described as a war council.

The Bird Guy, a few of the older folk from both sides, and Farm Girl sat on logs around an area of earth that had been scrapped and flattened down. The girl had picked up a stick and drawn a rough outline of the settlement in the dirt along with the main physical points of the landscape around it, including the mountain, forest, lake, and river. I came over and watched as she and Bird Guy walked around and around the dirt settlement, pointing here and making a mark there. They were evidently working on their strategy for the coming fight.

I studied their map and, after a while, it occurred to me

that they were getting it wrong. I could tell from their marks in the dirt that they seemed to think the attackers would come down the mountain and then spread out on a wide front to attack at a multitude of smaller points almost encircling the settlement. In theory, it was a good plan of attack. The long line meant that the attacking force could not be outflanked. The different points of assault would make it very hard to defend the entire settlement. From their marks, I could guess that their strategy involved a mobile form of defense, which would flow and ebb around the edge of the settlement to push back each attack as it occurred. I knew they were mistaken, however. I remembered, from the raid we had made on the tiny cluster of houses when I was in training, that it was just wrong.

I coughed but no one heard me. I then coughed louder and this time everyone turned to look at me. I held out my hand for the stick and the girl passed it over.

I stepped in front of their earth drawn settlement and took it in. First was the timing of the attack. I pointed at the sun above me, making sure not to look at it directly, and made a sloping motion with my hand until it was level with my waist. I waved my palm on an imaginary flat horizon. I pulled my hand up again and sank it gently down to my waist. I did the gesture a few times until the girl caught on and said something. Yes, sunset, that was when they would attack. Next, the method of attack. Assuming they followed a similar pattern of assault to the one I participated in, then they would not break up their force but rather keep it together in three concentrations consisting of a main group and two smaller side groups.

I bent down to their map and placed a thick X mark on the side of the mountain opposite the settlement. That would be their starting point. I then drew two stick arrows coming out from the X and stretching downward to arc around into either side of the settlement. The arrows represented the two smaller initial assaults. They served to pull attention away from the main force, mop up some of the stray defenders and, perhaps most important of all, sow confusion among the settlement. Next, I drew another thicker arrow coming down from the X directly at the settlement from the mountain side. That then, in a nutshell, was how they would attack. Two flanking motions followed by a straight heads-on assault by the main force intended to sweep aside any attempt at defense.

Bird Guy looked at the map, and after a while, nodded his head as if seeing the rationale behind my reasoning. He then held his two arms out wide, and to my surprise, flapped his hands up and down while cawing like a crow.

"Yes," I said, understanding his meaning. "I guess it does look a little like a bird, the flanks are the wing tips and the main attack is the beak. Which I guess would make us the worm."

He came to a stop, calmed down, and stared at the map again. He reached out for the stick, which I handed to him. He drew a thick straight line stretching from the two outmost houses that faced my mountain X and the main attack. He planted both feet firmly on the ground and then made the motion of pulling an arrow followed by swinging a club or axe. He pointed back to the line in the earth between the houses. He held the stick up in front of him. I got it and nodded. A defensive wall containing archers who would then resort to hand weapons if the enemy got closer.

He stared again at the map, tapped the two outer arrows, and looked up at me. How to deal with the two wide flanking movements? If not stopped directly, they could easily get around the settlement and come from behind to attack our main line. They would probably be significantly less in numbers than the main attack, but even a few men could cause havoc if they got into the settlement. Placing similar defensive lines out wide of the settlement was not feasible. That would split up our already small force and do little in reality as they could simply side-step any barrier we built. The flanking groups were meant to be small and mobile. They were meant to distract us, obscure their main attack, and generally confuse us. It was a trick really, nothing more. Looking at the map, I wondered if perhaps we should not try something along the same lines as well. I then had an idea about dealing with their flanking movements.

Chapter Nineteen

As it was getting toward evening, I went down to my uncle's house to check on him. I had not seen him all day. Along the way, I inspected the barricade we had all worked on throughout yesterday and today. The barricade ran across the open ground between the two houses at the outermost edge of the settlement facing the mountain. Previously, the mountain had always been a source of comfort to the inhabitants of the Lake Settlement, seeing in its dominant presence the strength of the land. Now, it had become a point of anxiety as we looked to it and waited for the attack.

The barricade itself was the height of a man's shoulder. We had been lucky in having so many animal pens around the settlement. We had pulled up the dry brush and branch fences from the pens to overlay them against each other. A series of thick posts, ripped out from one of the smaller huts, was added along the length of the barricade to reinforce it. At regular intervals, we had also set up points containing large pots of water and food wrapped in leaves for the sentries who now manned the barricade. They watched out for the arrival of our runners, waiting up on the mountain itself, returning with news of the attack. The houses on either end of the barricade had also been incorporated into the defensive line. The inhabitants had moved out, taking all their valuables, bedding, and furniture with them. I had ordered a hole to be knocked in the thatch roof of each house and a plank of steps placed inside to provide ready access to the rooftops. The archers who were to be stationed up there had brought up sacks and odd timber planks to make themselves more secure upper nests on the thatch.

The cattle and sheep we had brought into the center of the settlement and fenced in a new round stockade. This was divided into two sections with the larger side for the cattle and the smaller area for the sheep. The animals had been restless at first, jittery about being moved and being packed in together, but they had settled down eventually. The Lake People had taken that as a good sign. Finishing all the jobs had been hard work and everyone had pitched in. During the day, I had stood back and watched as the Forest People and the Lake People toiled together, shoulder to shoulder, from early light to dark, helping each other as needed. I thought that maybe, just maybe, if we could defeat Wolf Killer, then these two peoples would have a future together.

I reached my uncle's house and went into the warm, darkened interior. He was sitting up, poking at the fire and drinking from a bowl. His sons, two fine grown boys, were not there, and I guessed that they were probably out with the other youths still sharpening their axes or preparing the stockpiles of arrows. Their mother, whom I had never really known, had gone to join her ancestors a long time ago.

"I'm sorry, Wild Flower," he said on seeing me enter.

"For what, Uncle?" I asked, approaching the fire.

"I should have been the one, not you, who went to the River Settlement to avenge my brother. I was afraid, for myself and about Wolf Killer's retribution on all of us."

"You were concerned about your people," I said as a way of reassurance.

"You know, some people said your father should have been made leader here and not me."

"I heard that."

"I loved your father, I did, but he would not have made a good leader. The settlement needed continuity. Your father wanted to change everything in a great rush. He wanted to make these things better, but people didn't want that. They wanted stability. You can see that. You will make a better leader than your father would have, a better leader than I was. You understand that change must always come slowly for us."

There was a soft knock at the door, and a moment later, the shaman woman entered through the porch. She could go anywhere she wanted in the settlement. Who would refuse her? She came in smiling, but I was surprised to see her this late in the day. Should she not be up at the Stone House speaking to our ancestors and harrying them for their assistance in the imminent fight? I assumed, from what I had seen at the River Settlement, that the shamans of Wolf Killer were all atop their mounds right now imploring Yellow Face and White Face to wipe us from the land. She came forward and took a place by the fire.

"Wild Flower, I was happy to see you return to us safe."

"Thank you."

"And your boy with you."

"Yes."

"He's not really an ancestor, is he? Isn't that what you said to First Calf when you came back?"

"No, he is not one of our ancestors. He's just a man, I'm afraid. I don't know where he came from, but he did not return from the Grey Mist."

"No," she said, looking into the fire. "I did not think so. I was hoping at first he was, I really was, but how can he be? He is so ignorant of our ways and our words. It is a little disappointing, but it is what it is. Is it true then that you went to the River Settlement, where the Wolf People live?"

"Yes."

"How exciting. That must have been magnificent. I heard rumors the Wolf People are building a huge Stone House for their ancestors to live in, is that true?"

"Yes, right in the middle of their settlement."

"And it is big, bigger than our Stone House?"

"Yes, as big as a hill."

"Really, that big? I would dearly love to see that someday." She took a ceramic bowl from the side of the fire and poured in some water from the large house drinking jug nearby. She pulled out some dried plants from a leather pouch to mix in with the water. Next, with her foot kicking against it, she loosened one of the hearth stones and, using the leather pouch to pick it up, dropped the stone into the ceramic bowl. Once the heat from the stone had transferred to the water, she scooped it out and shoved it back in place. My uncle, falling asleep by the heat of the fire, snored gently.

"Their ancestors must be very powerful," she continued. "To live in a Stone House like that."

"I had not really given it much thought. If anything, I thought it was too big, too...gaudy."

"Did you?" she said as if amused by the notion that I

would have such an opinion on the matter. "Perhaps you don't understand its real purpose. Just think about it. What it means. The land of the Grey Mist is a reflection of our land. We live in our settlement here and in the Grey Mist, we will live in our ancestor's Stone House. Here the Lake Settlement is small and weak compared to that of the Wolf People, so our Stone House is small compared to theirs. It makes sense that in the Grey Mist, their ancestors must be more powerful than ours, as the Wolf Men are more powerful than we are."

"I don't really know," I said, beginning to wonder why she was talking on such things. It seemed odd that a shaman would slight the very ancestors she was meant to intercede with on behalf of the settlement, especially now.

"It makes sense," she reiterated, and gave the bowl a swirl to mix the contents. "Take this, girl. It will bring you back to yourself."

She reached around the hearth with the bowl. I took it. I brought it up to my face and smelled the earthy brown brew.

"I will have it later," I said. "I am rested enough."

"Take it now. It must be taken hot," she insisted.

"Later," I said, putting the bowl down.

"Don't you trust me?" she asked.

"No." I tipped the drink out onto the floor of the house.

She looked amazed at my actions. Then, with a loud screech, she threw herself up and across the fire, sending up a sparkle of sparks, and landed near me. She pulled out a flint knife and took a desperate, clumsy swing at me.

I easily stepped back to avoid the blade and brought a closed fist up to hit her full in the face.She fell back with a look of shock, both perhaps at the sudden pain of the blow and at the startlingly fact that someone had dared to touch a shaman.

"You stupid girl," she hissed, reaching up to feel the blood running from her nose. "Don't you see? You want to save us, but we are already condemned. We cannot win. The ancestors of the Wolf People are too strong. They control the Grey Mist, the same way Wolf Killer controls this land. We cannot fight them. Our only hope is to join with them so when we travel to the Grey Mist, they will accept us into their Stone House."

"You are forgetting your own ancestors," I said.

"They are as powerless there as we are here. Wolf Killer cannot be defeated. He wants to be leader of all the land and he will be. We have to side with him. Then we will be safe. Can't you see that? That's why I've been helping him, helping the Wolf People, as best as I can. For all of us. The Lake People, though, they don't understand, they will only submit if you tell them to. They will follow you."

"You helped Wolf Killer?" I said.

"Yes, but for the Lake Settlement. I've preparing the way for all of us in the Grey Mist. If you were a true leader, you would see that."

I had been wrong. First Calf was not the spy of Wolf Killer. She was. In hindsight, it made perfect sense. Of everyone in the Lake Settlement, she would have been the easiest for Wolf Killer to approach as she tended the Stone House all alone. Perhaps he had even sent one of his own shamans to slip through the forest unseen to talk with her.

After that, once she had been won over, it would have been a simple enough matter to contact her again. She could stay away from the settlement for days on end and no one would comment. She could also go anywhere she wanted to gather information. I wondered similarly if she had been somehow responsible for dragging down the morale of the Lake People. She had the ear of everyone here and it would not have taken too much to implant seeds of uncertainty among the Lake People. To grow into a harvest of doubt.

For that matter, how long had she been coming to the house of my uncle? Had she undermined him, making him believe in the weakness of the Lake People and, by contrast, the unstoppable strength of the Wolf People? Had she broken him down slowly bit by bit until he could no longer trust his own judgement?

"They told me about the Stone House they are building," she said. "They told me how magnificent it would be. They said my bones could be laid there if I helped them, all of our bones could be laid there if only we submitted to them. That's why I told them to attack your farm. I thought that once the Lake People saw Wolf Killer's power, they would bow before him. I didn't know they would kill your father, though. I told them to burn your house, that's all. I could not save your father, Wild Flower, but I can still save you. Your bones could go to their Stone House, if only you would bow to Wolf Killer."

"If you're the sort of company I would keep in their Stone House, I would prefer to wander the Grey Mist alone forever," I said, looking across at her. "You're a disgrace. You are wrong and, when we defeat him, you will see that. Now, get out of here, go up to the Stone House, and beg our ancestors for their help. Isn't that what you are meant to do? And if I see you down in the settlement again before this is all finished, I will send you to meet your ancestors personally. You can see what they think about your treachery firsthand."

The door to the house banged open and one of the younger boys ran in panting and pointing back through the entrance.

"They're coming," he said. "The Wolf Men are coming."

Chapter Twenty

I may not have spoken the language, but it was easy to know what was happening as the evening quietness of the settlement was suddenly broken. People, talking and shouting excitedly to one another, emerged from the houses and ran to man the barricade. The attack came earlier than I anticipated.

I picked up my axe and followed. I found a spot near the house on the right side of the barricade that gave me a clear view of the ground rising up to the mountain. The line along the barricade was quickly filling in as everyone in the settlement responded to the call to arms. I was nervous like the night before an important exam, although I tried not to show it. I was very much aware of my own breathing, in and out, and, at that moment, was intensely conscious of my surroundings—the feel of the axe handle, the knot in the timber in front of me, the call of a bird in the distant trees, and the smell of sweat from the people on either side of me.

Around me, I spotted many of the younger boys and girls I had been training yesterday and the day before. It seemed odd seeing them there, as if we had only been previously playacting, but now it was very real. And yet, all of them stared ahead at the mountain and did not flinch from their posts. I felt proud of them and wondered if that was how it felt to be a parent.

I scanned the line and saw Farm Girl at the other end of the barricade. She must have sensed my eyes on her because she turned and nodded at me. I wondered if she was nervous as well. Funny how events could drag up other memories, but I suddenly recalled my grandad years ago talking about a conference he attended in Berlin, or somewhere like that.

There had been a huge debate among the academics at

the conference about whether or not warfare in this period was mostly symbolic in nature. A lot of shouting between small bands of men, rather than involving actual physical combat. My grandad thought it was all nonsense. He said that warfare was warfare. Killing was killing. Standing behind the barricade, I had to agree with him. This felt a lot more than symbolic.

The archer on the roof of the house nearest me let out a soft bird call. I looked up to see him point away from the barricade. At first, I could not tell what he was pointing at, but then, when I peered harder into the darkness, I saw the wave of hunched grey shapes emerging from the tree line. It moved not as a collection of men, as I realistically knew it to be, but almost as a single creature creeping forward toward its prey. I thought again of Bird Guy's earlier impression. That was the main attack ahead, the beak of the bird, coming to peck us, the small worm.

I held my axe tighter and, almost to take my mind off it, whistled quietly to get the attention of the man on the roof. He broke off a low whispered conversation he was having with a second man at the side of the house, who in turn was passing on the information to the rest of the line, and looked down at me. I pointed my axe out left and right as to ask what was happening to the sides of the settlement.

He stared out where I indicated and then shook his head.

I was not sure if he was replying in the negative or did not fully understand that I was asking about the outer groups of defenders I had put in place. Only after a great deal of hand signals had I gotten them to understand where I wanted them to go and what I wanted them to do. They were important to countering the attackers' flanking movements that I knew, as we sat mesmerized by the main attack, were already coming down to strike at our exposed sides.

What was happening out there? I needed to find out. I stepped back from the barricade and trotted along its length to the side entrance to the house. I climbed up the plank ladder and pulled myself onto the roof thatch to lie low beside the man already there.

From the higher vantage point, I could observe the enemy more clearly. They were still some way off. I could see that their main attacking force was stretched out in a wedge shape from a front forward-most point back up the slope. The sight made the hair on my arms stand up. I remembered, though, that during our attack on the house cluster we had moved fast to maintain the element of surprise. The approaching dark lumps were coming on slowly, however, almost cautiously. Perhaps they guessed that we were well aware of their arrival or they reckoned that this settlement denoted a far bigger target than a small bunch of defenseless houses.

I stared out to the far right hand side but could not discern any movement there. Then, as I was looking on, I saw a single torch light appear some distance away from the tree edge. It was tiny and barely visible in the thin dusk light. The flame started to move up and down as the torch bearer had been specifically instructed to do so according to my plan.

That first light was followed by a second and then a third. I looked ahead of the lights, knowing that the torch bearers would not have lit up if they had not spotted some of the enemy nearing their positon. I could just about make out a grouping of shadows approaching the torches, but they stopped on seeing their appearance. The enemy might not have been that afraid of us, but they were scared of Will-o'-the-Wisps. Their plan of attack did not need to be stopped, just thrown into confusion. The appearance of some Will-o'-the-Wisps would achieve just that. How were they to know if the Lake Settlement was surrounded by marshland or not? After all, there was no Ordnance Survey or online maps in this era.

I looked to the left, expecting, waiting for, a second similar round of torch blots to appear, but there was only darkness. Something was wrong. They were not ready, they were not in position, or they had fled. The left flank of the attack was bearing down on us and there was nothing to stop the men from reaching the settlement. Nothing to stop them coming around to attack us from behind. I glanced down to the barricade below where the archers were readying their bows. I had to do something to help them.

I made up my mind.

I ran to the end of the roof and, judging the distance to be safe enough, jumped to land on the ground below. I set off, moving between the front of our barricade and the oncoming men in the direction of where I had showed the left hand group to position themselves.

I sprinted away from the houses and moved up the ascent to the harder gorse, heading toward the trees. I soon covered the ground and burst in on the group of mixed older and younger boys and girls. They were all anxiously standing around one of the boys, with his bow and quiver disregarded on the ground beside him. He was on his knees desperately trying to light a torch by blowing on a small lump of ember taken from one of the house hearths. The ember piece had clearly burnt out, as he was having no luck. They turned in alarm at my arrival and were obviously uncertain what to do now that the plan had failed. I knocked the ember piece from the boy's hands and instead swished a line through the air on either side of me.

As they scurried to form a positon around me, and with my eyesight now adjusted to the dim, I looked up the slope to see the attackers seeping from the darkness ahead. On spotting us, they pulled themselves up to full height, let out a screeching war cry, and broke into a run. They pounded down the slope toward us. They raised their axes above their heads. In a moment, without any time to think, they were almost on us. As one of the men bore down on me, I dug my rear heel into the ground behind me and bared my teeth at him. As he got closer, I could make out his full form beneath the thick wolf skin he wore. He was not an animal, after all, but only a mere man. I held my axe low and loose. I felt the blood pumping through my heart. I felt powerful. I had an intense desire to show this stranger, this bully, this man who wished me harm, that he could not beat me.

He brought the axe down as he was nearly on me, going for a straight-off killing blow to the skull. That was an amateurish move on his behalf. I raised my own axe, holding both the stone head and the end of the handle, so the middle shaft took the force of his blow. I felt the impact in the base of my spine.

He grunted and pulled his axe free for another try. As he was now exposed, I brought a knee up and caught him between his legs. He doubled over and I swung my own axe around to whack him on the side of the head. As he tumbled to the ground, I breathed in deeply. The fight had literally taken a few seconds at most, but it seemed as if time had slowed down. I looked around me to see that the two sides were engaged in close combat. I saw the boy who had been trying to light the torch struggling against one of the enemy. I crossed the space between us and brought my axe down on the man's shoulder. He crumpled to the ground with a shout as his hand went automatically to the pain.

A few of the attackers seemed to be drawing back from the engagement, unsure of what to do. They had not been expecting this. They were not expecting us to put up such strong resistance. Their leader, that man from the hall, had probably told them that this would be a walk-over. All they had to do was show their faces to make us give up. That was why they had come at us shouting and with axes raised. They believed the mere sight of them would cause us to frighten and yield. They were wrong.

I reached down to grab the fallen axe of the second man I had knocked out and held both axes aloft with outstretched arms to face another of the enemy. He was only a teenager, barely more than a child, and looked visibly shocked at my appearance. He dropped his weapon, turned and ran. In the next moment, the rest of attackers broke in panic and fled back the way they had come. As the youths around me shouted and cheered at their hard-won victory, I looked to the settlement below us where I could hear that the real battle had started.

Chapter Twenty-One

As the ancestor ran past our position, I immediately guessed his intention. I was holding my bow as I crouched down with my shoulder against the barricade so I saw him go by through a gap in the timbers. After he had disappeared into the darkness, I put him from my mind. He was on his own. I turned my attention back to what was happening in front of me. On the rise of the ground, the enemy was approaching. The watchers on the roof were softly calling down continual bearings about their numbers and positioning.

Crow was listening intently to everything while taking a few short glimpses over the barricade to see the situation for himself. We had agreed earlier that Crow, as the one with far more experience of leadership in fast moving situations, such as hunting and the intermittent fights over the years to defend his patch of forest, would take the lead on the defense of the barricade.

Crow gave a low shrill bird call, signaling for the archers to ready themselves. It was nearly time for us to draw. My father had taught me how to hunt using the bow, and I had accompanied him on the rare occasions he had taken time off from his farming chores to go into the forest in search of wild boar. It was not a pursuit I had really mastered, however. I was certainly not an expert shot as some of the other men and women in the Lake Settlement were and almost everyone from the forest seemed to be. However, for the sake of our defensive line, I was good enough. Of course, hunting boar was one thing. Deliberately killing a human being was another. Despite what I had said about New Water starting the fire at the hall of the Wolf People, everyone now seemed to believe I had tried to assassinate Wolf Killer and that I had only been stopped by his swift reaction. I knew, of course, that was not the whole truth. I had been near enough to strike, it was true, but Boar had given Wolf Killer ample warning in time to stop me. The question remained, though. If Boar had not been there, would I have carried through on my intent? Would I have plunged the blade into Wolf Killer's neck? I honestly did not know. The same question could be asked again at this moment. Was I a killer? Now, though, it was different. Wolf Killer had not known of my presence, but the men coming toward us must surely by now suspect that we were waiting for them. Still, they came on. They had decided to attack us. Therefore, did we not have a right to defend ourselves?

I looked through the gap in the barricade and saw what had gotten Crow's attention. The line of the hairy beast, which had been sluggishly approaching our positon, was getting nearer. It was beginning to break up into individual grey shapes. As they got closer, I saw these forms dissolve to be replaced by men wrapped in leggings with a fur coat over their back and head.

I almost felt sorry for them, especially those at the front who were about to die. These were to be their last moments before they joined their ancestors. Poor fools, dying for what? They had probably not even expected any proper form of defense. I wondered if Wolf Killer had told them that taking the Lake Settlement would be easy. A matter of running in and scaring the inhabitants into submission or, at the very worst, setting the houses alight to burn out the cowering families inside. If so, he had been wrong, because we intended to fight. I brushed aside my concerns for the men ahead of me as I reminded myself again that they were coming to attack my home.

We remained down, hidden from view, letting them come on. The closer they got, the higher our chances of hitting them, especially given the fading light. It was important, Crow had said, that our first volley of arrows was strong and fast to demonstrate to the rest of the men what their fate would be.

The advancing line was headed by a single leading man who was a few steps ahead of the rest. He continuously scanned the barricade and the house tops, looking for the slightest hint of danger. I could not make out the face of the man. He seemed too small in stature to be Wolf Killer. I wondered if it was his son. The man stopped and held up a hand, signaling his men behind to halt. He stretched up his head and listened. What his eyes could not see, he was trying to hear. We kept silent, however, and there was only the chirping of a distant bird in its evening song until Crow called again. It was the perfect moment to strike as the men were now motionless targets, which were much easier to hit.

We stood while the watchers on the house rooftops rose up into kneeing positions to join in the assault. I pulled back the already placed arrow and aimed. Crow had emphasized, again and again, that we were not to fire blindly. Even if we had to take our time, we still had to go for a kill shot. We did not have the arrows to waste.

I aimed at a young man standing directly opposite me. As the arrows around me flew through the air, hitting the attacking men who screamed and fell, I paused a moment, held my breath, and then let loose. The arrow left me going straight on before dipping a little to tear into the youth's thigh.

He brought a hand up in shock at the pain and felt the blood pumping from his leg as he collapsed onto his knees. As the survivors of the attack turned away, I saw another much older man notice the youth. He stopped to drag the youth up and helped him limp away with the others.

Behind them, they left the dead and wounded who groaned and writhed on the ground. Was that it? Was that their attack? I was about to shout out to ask Crow when the gloom in front of us lit up with a straight line of dazzling flames, which, in the now near darkness, appeared as bright and blinding as the rising Yellow Face.

"Down," Crow yelled.

A spray of burning arrows came from the light and struck the barricade with steady thuds. With our heads still bowed, a second rush of arrows landed.

I peered up at the rooftops of the houses on either side of us and saw that they too were receiving a number of the flaming missiles.

"Put the fire out," Crow shouted.

We hauled up the large ceramic pots of water we had been using for drinking and poured them over the side onto the burning arrows. A few arrows nearer the top were plucked out and thrown away. The men on the rooftops, where we had been expecting a fire attack, threw pots of water across the thatch. The water ran down the thatch, turning the small flames to hissing, and dripped to the ground below. All the while, more arrows, some burning and some not, were landing around us. I heard a shout as someone was hit. We kept at it, however.

Maybe the shaman had gone to ask our ancestors for help after all. Or maybe the stout old timbers holding the barricade together were too large to catch fire easily. Either way, we managed to put out most of the blazing arrows. The wood still smoldered in places, sending a veil of smoke up in front of us.

Even before we could pause to catch a breath, a second attack came. There was a huge, deep roar, sounding like thunder rolling down a valley, in front of the barricade. Then, it seemed to me as if the entire ground before our positon rose up as the enemy stood tall, and began moving toward us.

I realized that the first attack had been a mere probing jab to determine our position and strength. The man standing beside me swore softly and stepped away from the barricade, but I reached out and pulled him back in.

"Loose," Crow shouted above the noise.

We sent arrow after arrow into the approaching mass. I no longer had any concern at the welfare of the attacking men but fired again and again. I could see some of the attackers were falling, but the main body of men kept coming and those who fell were trampled underfoot.

I fired until I ran out of arrows. I then threw the bow to one side and took hold of my axe. The men were less than the length of a house away by now and approaching fast. I was terrified and wanted to run, but I held my position. I thought of my father and silently asked him for his assistance to help me survive the coming clash.

The pack of oncoming men then hit the barricade with a loud crash of wood, sending up a burst of dust and smoke amid the shouting and cries. An axe was swung over the top of the barricade at me by a screaming man. He missed and hit the wood. I brought my own axe down, cracking him on the top of the head. He fell away with a wail but was replaced by another man bearing a thick wooden cudgel that struck me hard on the shoulder. I winced under the pain and stumbled from the barricade. My attacker was then hit by the man I had pulled back into the line.

From my positon out from the barricade, I looked up and down the line. It had held against the Wolf Men's first on-slaught. The people of the Lake Settlement were standing firm, but I could see that the sheer number of attackers now pressing up against the barricade was causing it to bulge in the middle.

I recognized Wolf Killer among those at the center as he swung his club with deadly accuracy. He too had seen the bulge and was calling for his men to rally to him.

I shouted to the archers on the roof nearest me and pointed to the middle. They saw my signal and redirected their arrows into the thick knot of attackers there. The bulge eased for a moment under their fire, but was then renewed as Wolf Killer successfully pulled in more of the men around him against the weak spot. As those at the front of the attack went down, knocked away by the defenders or hit by arrows, they were replaced by those coming from behind. The defenders at that point were in contrast starting to thin out as we had no reserves to send in.

The missiles from the rooftop stopped and I knew, with a twisted feeling in my stomach, that they had finally run out of arrows. The attackers surged forward, causing the middle of the barricade to begin buckling in under the weight of the bodies, living and dead, now pushing against it.

If it broke, the remaining defenders in that section would be crushed underneath while the attackers would swarm in. They would have effectively split us in two, allowing them to hack away at our sides. If that happened, neither Crow nor I would be able to stop the defenders from fleeing. I looked to Crow, but he was fighting hand to hand and had not seen the danger. I thought for a moment, if only I had longer to de-cide, but I knew I had to do something. We could no longer hold the ground.

"Fall back," I shouted. "Fall back."

The defenders around me heard my shouts and repeated the order down the line. As they pulled back from the fight, the barricade in the middle broke inward and the swell of at-tackers collapsed forward onto one another. As they strug-gled up, we had enough time to break free and scurry back into the settlement.

There was only one place left to go, which Crow and I had already secretly agreed on if the worst should happen. We ran through the houses to the central animal pen. We climbed or fell over the fence to land among the frightened animals, which stomped and kicked out at the sudden violent intrusion. I stood and looked about me, trying to take in how many of us had survived and what state we were in. My shoulder was still aching.

Crow was quicker than me. He moved around the pen, giving encouragement and shouting orders. Those still able to do so, moved to form a defensive circle against the fence just as the first of the Wolf Men arrived between the houses and rushed into the space around us.

Wolf Killer appeared at the head of his men. He came forward slowly. He probably realized we had no more arrows left, but he was not stupid enough to risk getting hit by a well-aimed thrown axe. He walked around the pen, directing his men to certain positons and ensuring our encirclement was complete. Torches were lit and held aloft to form a ring of light around us. Along with the noise of the restless cattle and sheep behind me, the groaning of our wounded, and the crying of the younger defenders, the circle of light added to the crushing effect of the people now trapped in with the animals. I noticed one of my cousins was in here with us, a bloody gash across his forehead, and I wondered if perhaps my uncle and the shaman had been right. Perhaps Wolf Killer was too powerful to resist and perhaps we should have submitted. If we did not have our freedom, at least we would have had our lives. Would that have been enough? Wolf Killer finally came to a halt and looked out over scene before him.

"I am surprised," he shouted. "That you, nothing more than farmers and fishermen, put up such a good fight. You can be proud of yourselves, but it is over now."

Crow looked over at me and nodded. Wolf Killer was right, the fight was finished. It would be wrong to sacrifice our lives for nothing. My shoulder hurt as I pulled myself up straight.

"If we surrender," I called out in response, "will you swear on Yellow Face to let us live and not to take any reprisals?"

"Let you live," Wolf Killer said, shaking his head. "I am sorry, but I can't let any of you live. If we had taken the Lake Settlement without a fight, perhaps most of you could have survived, but now, you challenged me. I need to send out a warning to all the settlements on this side of the mountain. Go against me and this is what you can expect. I will burn you and this settlement to ash so the smoke will be seen for days to come. Then, they will know, the Wolf is here."

He shouted instructions and the circle of men around us moved in. The fence would not hold them for very long. At least the ancestor got away. At least he would survive. A pity, though, I would have liked to have known him more.

Chapter Twenty-Two

We were too late to help at the barricade. The broken wooden ruin lay on the ground amidst a scatter of bodies, some of whom were still moaning and moving. We did not have time to help them and, to be honest, there was little we could do for them. I brought my small group around the barricade and into the settlement. I could hear a loud commotion ahead so we clung to the sides of the houses as we moved deeper into the timber surroundings. On reaching the last structure, which faced onto the central area, I waved a hand for the group behind me to stop. I went ahead to the end of the wall alone and looked around the corner. A dense throng of the enemy, some holding torches, had their backs to me as they all focused on what was in front of them. I moved my head from side to side to get a glancing view through the press of men and saw that the surviving defenders of the settlement were surrounded within the cattle stockade.

I spotted a glimpse of Farm Girl.

She was shouting something over the stockade fence to someone, the leader of the enemy, I presumed. I was glad to see she was still alive.

I had to help them. I had to help her, but what to do? I weighed up the option of a direct attack. Myself and my small group of six teenagers hitting one part of the encirclement hard. Maybe the others trapped inside the cattle enclosure could join in and fight their way out. For that to work, however, I would have to somehow signal to them what the plan was, and there was no simple or quick way of doing that without giving away our own position. Besides, there were so many of the enemy that a direct attack may not have made that much of a dent. I needed a much bigger force to have any hope of success or, it occurred to me, I needed to convince the enemy I had a bigger force.

It was odd, but I then had an image in my mind of the white-and-black cat Pauline from school owned. One day, it had been cornered in the garden by a neighborhood dog and had arched up onto its feet to make itself look bigger. Pauline had rushed out from her house to help, but by then the dog had ventured too close and received a scratch from the cat's claws. It ran yelping from the garden. We needed to achieve a similar effect.

I returned to my group. They looked to me anxiously, waiting for leadership. I could understand their worry. For them, it was their mothers, fathers, brothers, sisters, and friends trapped in the stockade. Three of them still had bows. I nodded to the biggest lad with a bow, pointed to the roof of the house we were standing beside, and pulled back on an imaginary arrow. I then held my two open palms downward indicating he was to wait.

He nodded, getting my meaning straight away, and began hauling himself up onto the roof using an overhanging timber poking from between the thatch.

I then gestured to the other two archers and circled my finger in the air, drew the invisible bow again, and twirled my finger once more. I wanted them to spread out and find their own locations overlooking the enemy.

They moved off.

I took in the remaining group consisting of two boys and a girl. We needed to help, but I was not sure how. We could throw our axes, but it would be a one shot only and seemed a waste of a good weapon. And I still had no idea how to correctly throw an axe, or even if the axe head was sharp enough to cut through the hides the enemy wore.

If we wanted to support the archers, what we really needed was missiles of our own. But what? I saw the narrow side entrance to the house in front of me. There had to be something in there we could use. I pushed in the plank door and stepped into the interior. I looked around and spotted the floor hearth encircled by a row of fire hardened stones. It presented a perfect supply of ready missiles.

I pointed to the hearth, but then thought maybe they would think I wanted a fire started to cover the central area in a smoke screen. Not a bad idea, actually, but there was not enough time to start and fan a full scale blaze. So, instead, I went over and pulled up one of the hearth stones myself. Now was as good a time as any, I said to myself, to test if these people really believed that the dwelling hearth was a sacred special area of the house, as I had often heard my grandad say, or if it was just a stone circle with a fire in the middle. There were no shouts of protests from the any of them, so I yanked up the rest of the stones. I held up the bottom of my top and piled them into the hanging cloth like a child would collect shells at the beach to bring home.

The girl caught on quicker than the other two, and she came forward to help. Between us, we soon cleared all the stones and stepped out again into the night air.

Without any prompting from me, the two lads crossed the open ground to the nearest house and vanished inside, I guessed, to pull up their hearths or pick up whatever else they could lay their hands on.

I crept forward to the corner of the house again. I glanced up to the archer who had put himself into a good firing position near the front gable end of the roof. He was waiting above me, his head hanging over the side, for my signal. I watched until the two lads appeared from the house opposite us and, loaded down with their own missiles, went to the end of that house. We were ready. I hoped my plan would work.

I thought of the lads I had trained with at the river settlement. Despite everything, I hoped they were safe and, for their sake, none of them were in the crowd. I assumed they had been involved in the action tonight, but wondered if they had known I was here. If so, had they had any qualms about the attack? Still, I remembered how they had all stood back when we raided the houses and done nothing as the poor man there was about to be executed. They had not stepped up then, so probably never would.

I nodded at the archer.

He raised the bow, took careful aim, and let the arrow fly. As soon as it hit the man he had targeted, who fell with a low shriek, he was pulling another arrow free to aim again.

I picked out a smooth rock from my pile, swung back my fist, and hurled it as hard and as accurately as I could. To my immense surprise, it hit one of the men in front of me squarely in the center of his back.

He hopped forward, shouting in pain, and spun about to determine where the rock had come from. He then noticed the other man who had fallen with an arrow sticking from his lower shoulder. He shouted the alarm and others near him looked to see what the trouble was.

The girl beside me threw a stone and managed to hit a different man directly on his forehead. We then slipped away from the house corner before they could spot us. We raced along the length of the house, nearly banging into the archer as he dropped from the roof to the ground in front of us. He grinned at me, as if enjoying himself, and ran to find a new position.

The girl and I set off in the other direction to a nearby house. My aim was not as good as hers, that was obvious, but I still landed a few more decent shots from there. From our second location, I saw another arrow spring from a different angle, taking down another one of their men.

More and more of the men at the edge of the encirclement around the animal pen were starting to turn, weapons held tight, looking out into the dark settlement, which, perhaps it now seemed, had suddenly encircled them. The flaming torches were held up higher as they tried to determine who was attacking them. Of course, that only prevented them from seeing us even more as they were blinded by the contrast between the light and the dark.

After a few moments, there was a parting in the crowd and I saw their leader come forward to sort out the turmoil going on behind him. I could not have arranged it better, but at that moment an arrow struck the chest of the man standing next to him. The leader scanned the rooftops, guessing its source, but was unable to place its exact origin. There was a growing murmur from his now increasingly jittery men. They were obviously asking each other if there was another force of defenders they had not counted on. Maybe they had been deliberately tricked into venturing to the tight heart of the settlement and so had fallen into a trap of their own?

The leader shouted orders, doubtlessly directing his men to set up an outer defensive line. It was too late, however. With perfect timing and clearly seeing the attack taking place, there was a mighty roar as the fighters inside the cattle enclosure seized the opportunity and came over the fence with weapons held high.

As the enemy scattered in alarm at this new threat, Bird Guy let his axe fly with the accuracy I lacked straight at the leader of the enemy. It hit him on the back of his head, sending him stumbling forward a few feet. Not a killing blow, but enough to stun him and more importantly, throw his men into further confusion.

I let the last of my stones fall to the ground, gripped my axe, and ran at the nearest man holding a torch. He saw me and dropped the torch to scramble for his own weapon, but he was too slow. I brought the axe head directly down onto his neck and he twirled around with a shout before collapsing.

I heard the young girl behind me scream in apparent rage as she flew forward to join in the attack. It was too much for the enemy. Confronted on both sides, with arrows still flying into them and their leader wounded, some of the men at the verge of the encirclement were the first to take flight. They bolted for a safe passage between the houses.

Once it began, there was no stopping the panic. The fear jumped from man to man and became a far greater enemy than we were. More and more turned around to flee until it became an all-out rout. Soon, the entire force of the enemy was streaming away from the central area, pushing into and hitting out at each other in their bid to escape.

We chased them as best we could, swinging our weapons and shouting with a blood-tinged glee at seeing the enemy so. Finally, as I reached the end of the settlement, I came to a stop and leaned onto a fence post to rest. Ahead of me, the attackers, still pursued by a number of the settlement folk, were crossing the outer most fields to vanish into the night air from where they had come.

I felt someone touch my arm and I turned with my weapon ready. It was only Farm Girl, though. She was smiling and talking to me. I found tears swelling up at the corners of my eyes for the sheer relief and joy of the occasion.

She threw her arms around me. I did not know if I kissed her first, or if she kissed me, or maybe our lips just meet by accident, but I felt the warmth of her breath close to me and I kissed her back. The swell of victory, and our first embrace, emerged together.

Chapter Twenty-Three

After the joy of triumph came the rush of total numbing exhaustion and the feeling of being absolutely flattened by the events of the night. After the retreat of the Wolf Men, when we chased them from our home across the fields, we had all just stood and looked at each other, stunned that we had won when it had seemed so definitely helpless.

I found the boy on the edge of the settlement. I was over-joyed he was still alive and thankful he had come back for us. Maddeningly, I could not thank him for what I knew he had done. We embraced and kissed. A kiss of victory, shared hardship and what else, of love, I did not know. It seemed natural, obvious even, that we should kiss. We held our embrace for a long few moments until, caught up in the still beating excitement of the crowd and the occasion, we parted and I drifted back to the central area of the settlement.

Some of the people there were crying in happiness or sorrow, some were laughing, some stood alone while others were kneeling silently beside those that had fallen. Seeing them like that, I reminded myself that despite what they had just achieved, these people were not hardened warriors. They were, as Wolf Killer himself had put it, just farmers and fishermen. I realized they needed leadership now more than ever.

I shook myself out of my trance. There was much work to be done. The wounded had to be cared for, fires lit to warm ourselves, while food and water had to be brought out and shared. I doubted the Wolf Men would return this night, but still, as a precaution, we would need to set up a ring of sentries around the settlement to keep a watch out.

I called to Crow and asked him to see to the guards. He looked at me, as if not understanding or hearing my words, so I repeated the instructions and he then came back to his own self. As he went off calling out to his own people, I pulled together a few of the Lake People and began to organize our settlement again.

In the first morning light, as Yellow Face rose to greet us, I ordered a funeral pyre to be built down by the lake using the pieces of the broken barricade. Once it was ready, we gathered up our dead. I would have preferred to wait until the old folk and children had been brought back from their camp, but I knew the bodies would quickly begin to smell over the coming day.

After every one of our dead had been respectfully laid out side by side, together in death, I nodded to the shaman woman who went forward with the flame she had brought down from the Stone House. She thrust the torch into the tinder at the bottom of the pyre. As the tinder crackled and the fire caught, spreading through the base of the structure to the bigger pieces of wood on the top, I took out the leather wrap from under my clothing. I rolled it open and picked up the heart of my father. Pushing the wrap and the arrowhead back into its concealment, I went forward with the heart to place it in the topmost part of the pyre. I stood back to watch as the flames embraced it.

Those around me, the survivors, cried for their beloved ones. We had lost so many. I cried too, quietly in my heart, for my father who had died defending his home as well.

Later that night, when the fire had cooled, we would collect the ash and burnt bone fragments to bring up to the Stone House so our dead could find their way home. My father too would come home through the Grey Mist. Afterward, we would have our funeral feast here in the settlement. We would eat and drink, and those that wanted could tell a tale of their part in our victory. On the hill, our ancestors would give another feast in the Stone House for their newly arrived members.

I had ordered the enemy dead to be left near the tree line. We mended the cuts of their wounded as best we could and fed them. As light broke, they started to limp home through the forest. I stopped one of the men and told him that if the Wolf People wanted their dead, they should send an emissary to collect the bodies. If they did not, I would order them to be burnt later.

I had searched among the dead, but neither Wolf Killer nor his son was among them. They had escaped presumably back to the River Settlement. The news of this victory would spread to other settlements, and I suspected that even if Wolf Killer remained in power, he would have his hands too full to bother us for some time to come. Who knew? Maybe this defeat would weaken him permanently. Perhaps his own people or children would turn against him, and that would be the end of Wolf Killer. In any wolf pack, there was always a younger and stronger wolf waiting to challenge the dominant male.

Even with him gone, however, there would be other threats to our home. If not him, then someone else would come along. My uncle was right, the land was changing and we needed to change with it. We could not be so innocent anymore. We could no longer be a settlement of just fishermen and farmers. We needed to become stronger so we could defend ourselves.

I half listened as the shaman wailed a ritual lament. Once she had finished with her duties over the coming days, I would force her to bring in one of younger girls so she could be trained as her replacement. The shaman had joined her axe with the enemy and, when the time was right, she would have to be exiled from the settlement. From now on, we could not afford to allow such weaknesses to persist.

After a while, I could bear the heat of the fire no longer. I turned away and walked up to the houses. I looked ahead to see Crow bringing my mother down to the lake. On seeing me, she ran forward and gave me a tight embrace. She looked well-fed and rested. As Crow had said, living in the forest had seemed to agree with her.

"Thank you, Crow," I said. "Have you mourned your dead?"

"Yes, they have been taken back to the forest where they were born."

"And Boar?"

"I did not find him among the dead or wounded."

"And now?" I asked. "You'll go back to your beloved

trees?"

Crow looked up to our settlement where people were already cleaning away the signs of the fight. Life still went on. The animals still needed to be tended, the crops cared for, and the food supply ensured for the next winter.

"I don't know," he said. "The ways of the Forest People are coming to an end, I can see that. The older ones still cling to them and will not give up the forest, but we must change, to ensure that our children can grow and prosper. If we leave it too late, we will never be able to adapt."

"You are going to become farmers?"

"I don't know yet. Maybe."

"As I said, we can help you, show you how to plant and look after the animals."

"Maybe."

"You can always come live with us. We need to grow our settlement, become bigger. Your men and women would be a welcome addition."

"I must talk with my people first," he said. "It's not a decision that can be rushed."

"No, I guess not."

I had some difficulty in seeing Crow as a farmer, but, like me, he would make the tough decisions that had to be made.

"And the other thing we talked about?" he asked.

I knew he was referring to his marriage proposal. I had had no time to ponder on it since he brought it up. And to be honest, I had not made up my mind one way or the other. I cared for Crow and I believed he cared for me, but was that enough?

"I am still thinking about it," I said.

He nodded as if that was an answer in itself. I watched him leave and begin the trek back to the forest. I took my mother's hand and explained gently that I had placed her husband's heart among the dead and he would be all right now.

She was happy at that thought and held my hand tight.

I needed to look after her now. We could move in with my uncle for the time being and then next spring we would build our own house on the edge of the settlement. There was a lot of rebuilding to be done. I remembered the timber palisade from the River Settlement and wondered if such a thing would be possible here. It would take a long time to construct, but it would be worth it to defend the settlement. Then, when others came to take what was ours, they would have to ask how many men were they willing or able to sacrifice? Later, when the mourning was over and the people had returned to their lives, I would have First Calf call an assembly. We would discuss everything that needed to be done under my guidance.

I saw the ancestor coming toward me and I knew he had come for the arrowhead. I murmured to my mother that I would return later and left her to join him. He nodded at my approach and, to my surprise, took my hand in his.

We walked away from the houses, the settlement, and the other people. We went up to the forest edge. We sat on the grass and looked out over the scene below us. From up here, aside from the plume of smoke down by the water, it seemed as if everything had already returned to normal.

I leaned in against him and he kissed me again, a long kiss, but this time it was a kiss goodbye. I did not know where he had come from and where he would return to, but this was not his land or his people. There was one thing I needed to know, however, before he left.

"My name is Wild Flower," I said, pointing to my chest. "Wild Flower."

He did not understand me at first, but after I repeated it several times, he seemed to get my meaning for he tapped his own chest.

"Heen Ri," he said. "Heen Ri."

So that was his name. I wondered what it meant in his language. I took out the leather wrapping and gave it to him. We sat for a long while there just being together as birds flew overhead and Yellow Face smiled on the land. It was going to be a beautiful day.

I then heard my name being shouted. My mother was coming up the hill, calling me down for breakfast. I stood up and went forward a few steps to answer her, thinking that the boy could join us for one last meal, but when I looked back, he was gone. The only thing left was the small flint arrowhead lying on the grass.

Chapter Twenty-Four

It was when I saw the girl with her mother than I knew I could not stay. I had to go home to my own family. I saw the look of joy on the older woman's face upon seeing her daughter safe and sound. My dad and grandad were probably worried sick about me, and I could not put them through the pain of not knowing what had happened to me. I owed it to them to return home safe and sound as well.

I took her hand amidst all the comings and goings of the people around us. Her hand felt warm. We went up above the settlement. I was not sure which one of us brought the other to the tree line, but it was very pleasant to sit there and watch the houses below. At the lake, the huge fire burnt, sending a pillar of smoke into the air.

I did not attend the funeral, as I felt it would be inappropriate. These were not my folk. They deserved to be left alone in their grief. As I looked down on the fire, I could not help but wonder how long it would burn. How long did it take fire to consume a human body, to reduce their remains to black ash?

These people had sacrificed so much in defense of their home and way of life. And yet, already I could see they were returning to some sort of normality. A group of men were even now taking the cattle out to the fields. I guessed that soon they would bring the children and older people home again. Undoubtedly, some of the children would have lost parents and the older folks may have lost children. They too would have to mourn for their missing family members, and then, as it always had, life would go on.

I kissed her and felt the warm press of her body.

She looked at me and said something.

At first, I did not focus on her words, assuming I would not understand what she was saying as always like before.

Then, however, she repeated a particular set of words over again while holding a finger up to herself.

"Taal Fal," she said, or at least that is what it sounded like to me.

I understood.

"Henry," I replied. "Henry."

She seemed satisfied with the answer and handed me the leather cloth that contained the arrowhead. I pulled away from her, feeling sad at the thought of having to leave. I wondered if I would ever be able to come back, but I knew either way I had to return home.

I had my own people who needed to be looked after. And, I missed my dad terribly. I wanted to talk to him again and, I don't know, look after him better. I wanted to take some of the burden off his shoulders of worrying about me constantly and say to him that it was going to be all right. I could look after myself. It was time for him to relax, begin to enjoy his life once more and, who knows, even start dating again. Maybe we should take that holiday in New York he had always talked about. The whole of his life had been consumed with looking after me, the house, and his job after Mum's death. There had been nothing left for him. I wanted that to change when I got home.

There was a shout below us and the girl stood up to look. Her mother was coming up the hill toward us, saying something in that strange language of theirs.

This was the moment for me to leave. No tears or hugging. I wanted to keep our last time together just as it was. I unwrapped the leather cloth and looked down at the arrowhead. I pondered in amazement that such a small thing had caused so much to happen.

I wondered again if this would work. Was I right or would I spend the rest of my life here with her by the lake learning to be a farmer? Perhaps that would not be such a bad life. And, to be honest, if I did not have Dad and Grandad back home waiting for me, I would have been very tempted to wrap up the arrowhead again and forget about it. Bury it up by that tomb on the hill to let some future archaeologist dig it up. That was not a real option, though. I had to try to get home.

I reached out and touched the flint with my finger. The

settlement and the girl disappeared, and I was back in my grandad's office. It was smaller than I remembered. The artificial straight lines of the desk and shelves, the books and the organization of the room seemed a little out of place after being so long in the world of the settlement by the lake.

"Henry," a voice said behind me.

I turned and saw my father sitting in the desk chair, staring dumbfounded at me. He looked older, more haggard, and I noticed he had not shaved in days. I wondered how long I had been gone. Had the same amount of time gone by here as in the other place, or had there been a difference in the time that had passed?

"Henry," he said again.

"Dad."

"Is that you?"

"It is."

"You're home," he stated.

"I am."

"Where have you been?" He jumped up from the chair and crossed the room to squeeze me tight. "You smell terrible."

I laughed and that broke the tension. To my surprise, I saw tears in his eyes. I realized at that moment, despite all the times we had fought and all the times he had been hard on me, exactly how much my father truly loved me.

"Dad, it's great to see you again."

"Where have you been? Everyone is out looking for you. We thought you had run away or been kidnapped or something. I called all your friends and our relatives and anyone we could think of. A girl at your school even set up a website looking for information. The police have even begun searching for you. No one could find any trace of you. It was like you vanished from the face of the earth. And what are you wearing?"

"Dad, I don't know where to begin. I went somewhere else. I helped a lot of people and I met a girl."

"You were with a girl, is that where you have been?"

"Kind of."

"A girl," he exclaimed. "But where are your clothes?"

"This is what I had to wear."

"Was it a fancy dress party or something?" he said, and

then shook his head. "I don't know, but it doesn't matter. You're back now, that's the main thing. I must have fallen asleep and woken up when you came in. I have to ring everyone, ring the police station for starters, and tell them you're safe. I need to get my phone. And a girl, imagine. I will have to tell everyone you ran off with a girl." He hugged me again and practically leapt from the room in his excitement.

I was left alone not quite sure what to do with myself. I then remembered the arrowhead. I walked over to the glass case behind the desk and saw that the door to the case was shut, although not as tightly, meaning the lock was still probably broken.

I stared down at the arrowhead, which was still there. Pure white except for that black lightning strike running down its center. That small piece of stone had so much history attached to it, even more now than when I first went near it, and I wondered what would happen if I was to touch it again? Would I go back? Would I see her once more?

The door opened and my grandad was there. He looked at me and broke into a wide smile. He came forward and, again to my total surprise, pulled me in close to him. In my absence, all the men of the family had become huggers.

"Henry, my dear, dear boy, we are so happy to see you," he said, and then looked at me sternly. "And where were you? Your poor father was worried sick. I just met him in the kitchen. He said you ran off with a girl to a party or something like that. What is he talking about?"

"There was a girl, that's true."

He then seemed to notice the clothes I was wearing for the first time and reached out to rub the end of my sleeve between his fingers.

"A girl, really," he said. "You are dressed very oddly for meeting a girl. Is this animal hide? What animal is this made from? Did you make this yourself? Where exactly did you get your costume?"

"I...listen, let's talk about it later. I need to have a shower first and change."

"Your father brought over some of your clothes," he said. "For when you showed up. They're up in the guest room."

"Great."

"Ran off with a girl?" he repeated.

"I guess so, that'll be the story."

"Yes, well, if you insist, Henry. You know I would never doubt you. It's just your clothes seem so lifelike, so well-made. They seem almost real."

"Well, Grandad, what can I say?"

"Best to say nothing," he said.

"Exactly, now I really need to have that shower. After that, it sounds like I have lot of explaining to do to a lot of people."

"True, and Henry?"

"Yes?"

"If you ever need to talk, I am always here for you. You know that, don't you?"

"Thanks. Perhaps we should talk more. I reckon I could even tell you a few things now."

"Such as?"

"Well, for starters, I have been thinking about warfare in the Neolithic period quite a lot."

"Really," he said as his eyebrow arched up in bewilder-ment.

Epilogue

The office was large and fronted by a huge window that stared down on the town and university below. The wall opposite the window was taken up by a single glass shelf containing a row of priceless ancient finds of various origins. A white-and-blue dragon vase from China, a small statue of a standing figure from the Middle East, and a decorated drinking horn from Central Europe. The rest of the room was bare except for a single sleek desk and chair currently occupied by a man staring at a compact wall of monitors in front of him on the desk. The screens showed a complex spread of trading information and news feeds. There was a soft buzz in the air.

"Yes," he said.

"Sir, sorry to disturb you. Dr. FitzGerald is here. She says she has found 'it', but will not specify what 'it' is exactly. She said you would know."

"Send her in." He waved his hand and the monitors went blank.

A moment later, the double door at the end of the office opened and a middle-aged redheaded woman walked in carrying a black case.

"We found it," she said. "You were right. You said we just had to keep looking and we would find the evidence we needed."

"Show me."

She lifted the case up onto the desk and flipped it open. Inside, nestled carefully in a soft padded frame, was the partial remains of a broken and battered smart phone.

"Where?" the man asked.

"The excavation of the new site, the Neolithic house."

"You dated it?"

"Yes, it was found with a fence post. I managed to obtain

a date from a fragment of the timber using our own facilities. I also sent out a priority blind test to Holland and South Africa. They all came back with the same results. The timber piece is, approximately, six thousand years old."

"You're sure the phone was in its original context. It did not fall from someone's pocket? One of the students on the excavation maybe?"

"No, I excavated it myself. There is no doubt in my mind. It has been sitting in the same spot since the Neolithic period."

"You informed no one else?"

"I told the students it must have been dropped by one of the university staff when they surveyed the area last year."

"And they believed you?"

"Of course, why wouldn't they? Tell me, how did you know we would find something like this eventually?"

"Good work, Dr. FitzGerald," the man replied, ignoring her question. "Your funding is now guaranteed for the rest of your career."

"I don't care about more funding," she said. "You know what I want."

He looked up from the case across the desk at her.

"Don't get ahead of yourself, doctor. We still have some way to go. I need to have my people examine the phone. Undoubtedly, it is severely damaged, but with the technology we have here, we should be able to get some information from it."

"And then?"

"The first thing we need to do is find out who owns it. Then we need to know how they did it and if they can do it again. And bring others back with them. After all, whoever can access the past, owns the future."

The End

About the Author

Gerard Mulligan

Gerard Mulligan studied archaeology and wrote his doctorate on Neolithic Ireland. He has travelled here and there but is now firmly rooted at home.